Walking On Water

The Ripple Effect

By

Bobby Ferrel

Cadmus Publishing
www.cadmuspublishing.com

DEDICATION

For My Brother
And
In Loving Memory Of
Our Beloved Grandmother
Benina Luna Ferrel
We Love and Miss You, Ma'!!!

When the disciples saw him walking
on the sea, they were terrified. "It is a
ghost," they said, and they cried out
in fear. At once [Jesus] spoke to them,
"Take courage, it is I, do not be afraid."

Matthew 14:26,27

CONTENTS

CHAPTER ONE

Angelica's luxurious, long, black hair was in disarray, wet from sweat and matted to her butterscotch complexion. Her pretty face and supple cheeks were flushed as she expelled every bit of oxygen from her lungs, belting out an ear-piercing scream, "Uhhhh!"

"One final push," were the words she heard spoken from the soothing tone of Dr. Mona Hernandez.

Clamping down on Christopher's hand with all of her might, she took a deep breath and then did as instructed. Christopher winced as his wife crushed his poor fingers.

"She's out," exclaimed the doctor. As a professional, Mona was expeditious in cutting the umbilical cord and placing the baby on a nearby table where the awaiting nurse was.

Angelica was out of breath, screams, and fatigued. Quiet reverberated throughout the cold hospital room. Then suddenly the heavens opened up and the sound of an angelic choir could be heard from the cries of a newborn coming to life.

Christopher leaned down to kiss his exhausted wife on her damp forehead, his full beard soaking up the beads of sweat that had accumulated at her perfectly arched brows like a sponge. Then he spoke softly into her ear, "You did great, mi amor."

After the nurse had cleaned and wrapped the newborn in a pink satin blanket, Dr. Hernandez brought the baby over to Chris, presenting him with his daughter. "You are the father of a healthy, beautiful baby girl."

"Proud father," Chris replied. Cradling his little angel as he stared into her hazel, tear drop eyes being illuminated by the golden hue of her newborn skin. He was astonished to see she had a full head of short, wavy, black hair. Bending down to place her into Angelica's awaiting arms, he whispered, "She has your eyes, mi amor."

Dr. Hernandez inquired, "What name ultimately made the curtain call?"

"She's our little piece of heaven, so we chose Nevaeh," Chris said with a smile.

"I see, heaven spelled backwards. Well, that is clever and she certainly is a blessing. Now will you please excuse me? I have another patient expecting down the hall. Once again, I'm so glad you two finally have your long overdue bundle of joy."

In unison they replied, "Thank you, Mona," as the doctor exited the room.

Lingering on the doctor's last remarks, Chris couldn't help but replay in his mind the emotional heartbreak the miscarriage had caused four years into their marriage. Wanting so badly to have a child and start a family, that miscarriage had left a deep, painful scar on both of their hearts. Now six years after enduring that heartache and a trillion prayers later, they were elated to be proud parents, basking in this joyous, monumental moment.

✦ 4 ✦

CHAPTER TWO

A Mexican American growing up in Austin, Texas proved to be a daunting task for Christopher. Having had a start out in life on a rough road, Chris developed anger issues as he continued to roll with the punches.

Being a junior, Christopher only carried his father's name, never getting the chance to know him, or his mother, for that matter.

It was at the tender age of two that Chris was left with his grandmother on his mother's side. His parents loved Tejano music and on that night they attended an Intocable concert. All Christopher ever knew was that they never made it back to grandma Rosalee's home to pick him up.

That night as everyone exited the venue, a throng of innocent people were blindsided with a barrage of bullets flying from a fully automatic assault weapon.

The finger on the trigger was attached to a scrawny, 20-year-old, self-proclaimed, white supremacist. His fire red ratty hair draped over his acne-riddled face. His racist beliefs and hatred-fueled doctrine had enabled his actions that night. He ultimately shot 22 concert goers, injuring 14 and leaving eight deceased. Chris would later learn that his father was shot multiple times in the back trying to shield his mother. From that day on he was left in the care of grandma Rosalee, whom he called Ma', because she wasn't his mother, but she most certainly was his mom.

Ma' had flowing, long, black hair with a streak of silver running down the right side. She had the kindest deep brown eyes that stemmed from her loving heart. Ma' had raised two children, her eldest son, Eddie, and daughter Andrea. Ma' was a beautiful, strong Latina, raising her children alone after her husband passed away from a work-related accident at the railroad company he worked for. Ma' would receive his pension plus a settlement check from the company due to their negligence in the cause of the accident that killed her husband. Along with the life insurance, she was able to pay off her home and live comfortably.

Being that Andrea didn't become pregnant with Christopher until eight years after her father's death, Christopher would miss out on meeting his grandfather also.

His uncle Eddie was overseas serving in the military. He was a Marine and Chris would see him from time to time with years in between, until a knock came to the front door early one Monday morning. Two Marines immaculately dressed in uniform informed Ma' that her son had died an honorable death in combat.

Two things Chris learned in that moment were that life is short and death is inevitable.

He vowed from that day forth to always take care of Ma'.

Christopher's father was originally from California, leaving him estranged from that side of his family. Ma' did her best to give him a proper upbringing. With her age and health deteriorating, she would often bring Christopher to St. Peter's Catholic Church to have Padre Perez mentor and coax him into becoming a respectful, honest, and God-fearing man.

Padre Perez was newly appointed as parish priest. He had received his calling early on and now at the age of 33 he was pastoring the flock at St. Peter's. The family priest Father Gene had retired due to his age and debilitating, Parkinson's disease taking a toll on him. He would always be remembered for his light blond hair and mustache.

School was Christopher's Achilles heel with him excelling academically in science but flunking all other classes. He even failed Spanish class although he spoke fluently with Ma' at home. He just didn't take his work seriously. Instead, he would read books and science magazines under the guise of the classroom textbook.

Perceived by the other Hispanic boys as a nerd and science geek, his hefty glasses did not help the charge against him and got him teased for not playing sports and always reading. That's when fighting became the new normal. Timid at first until he let the pent-up anger from having lost his parents and constant bullying get the best of him. In eighth grade he came home with broken glasses and what would be his first and last black eye.

Upon seeing his face, Ma' put him in the car and drove to see Padre Perez. Refusing to baby him, she went to pray her rosary in the front pew, allowing Padre to teach him to cope with his anger.

Entering high school, Christopher had stretched to five feet and nine inches with a medium build, replacing his glasses with contacts and sporting braids down to his jaw line, alluring all the girls to his handsome face. Ma' had spent over an hour battling to braid his curly hair while he sat enjoying her company.

It was during that conversation that Ma' had revealed her secret to having such a beautiful garden and immaculate rose bushes. Ma' nonchalantly explained to Christopher that you must speak to the plants. Tell them they are strong, and they will grow to display their beauty. Encourage them through words, and also from time to time give them a little beer to drink. Seeing Christopher's face from hearing the information she gave she knew it would require deeper insight. She revealed that it served two purposes. First of all, it would help get rid of some of the beer and have less for grandpa to drink, and secondly, just a little would go a long way, keeping the plants merry and blooming.

Those hair braiding sessions with Ma' would be short lived due to the fact that Christopher was now perceived as a pretty boy. Surrounded by gang infestation and jealousy, it wasn't long before the fighting resumed, leaving Christopher no alternative but to cut his hair to keep it from being pulled during the fisticuffs.

Short on top, laid down with a taper on

the sides and back was his new style. Pretty much a loner, Christopher went about the day just trying to learn. He would routinely run three miles on the treadmill in the garage, keeping him long winded, along with doing push-ups and sit-ups for an hour after the miles to sustain his medium build physique.

Christopher dated a handful of girls, but the relationships were short lived due to the fact he never really put the time or effort into making a serious, long-standing commitment. He was more focused on taking care of Ma'.

Having always taken a liking to Padre Perez, the young, clean shaven, charismatic priest with movie star good looks, was upbeat and always had words of wisdom for him. Chris would listen intently to the seeds Padre Perez would sow. Born with a good heart mixed with wanting to make Ma' happy is what kept Chris from flying off the handle.

Oftentimes Chris would get a one-on-one with Padre Perez while Ma' would pray her rosary. What opened Christopher up to Padre's wisdom early on was when he explained the senseless attack on his parents.

Padre Perez had described racism as a direct effect of perception, simply stating that your skin is only the God-given clothing for your soul. Regardless of the color of your skin, our souls are one in the same. Now would you hate a man because he dressed funny in your opinion? If his shirt was wrinkled, would you want to bring harm to him? Some people dress in high-end fashion while others can barely afford to purchase attire from Walmart. Should these hard-working people be thought of any less on account of the price of the clothes they wear? Everything begins and ends with the soul and perception. Your soul is clean and pure until you decide to taint it, and even then, you can repent and come to Jesus to be renewed.

People's perception must be altered to attain a room in the Heavenly Kingdom. No man puts on an expensive suit without a shower and a shave. The same is to be said about a woman and her dress. You desire to be clean and presentable. It is the same with your soul. We need to see people for who they truly are. If someone rubs you the wrong way, leave it with that individual and not the same race of people.

Before you can truly love someone you must look through a soulful lens. We are called to pray for discernment so that we may love people fully and allow blessings to manifest.

Every soul yearns to be pure and every eye wanting to see out of a clear lens. It is up to God's children to illuminate the light from within those people with our actions. Allowing the word of God to live through us will eradicate hate and remove the wicked stye clouding up their eyes, bringing about a clear vision of love.

That was one of the early on lessons that Padre Perez taught Chris that left him captivated and wanting more. Entering Ma's house you could tell Ma' was a devout Catholic praying her rosary daily for the unborn children, to stop wars and violence, and to bring peace to all of God's people. She had statues of Jesus and the blessed Virgin Mary in her living room and bedroom, instilling in Christopher a strong Christian compass to guide him along his journey through life.

With Ma' having a green thumb, which showed in her flourishing garden and immaculate rose bushes, she took great delight in passing down the care and understanding for horticulture. Ma's routine every morning consisted of her drinking a black cup of coffee at 5:30 a.m. and making fresh tortillas soon after. Christopher would be in the garden by 6:45 a.m. to pick jalapenos so she could prepare chile for breakfast.

Christopher delighted in Ma's home cooking just as much as he enjoyed those times in the garden, soaking up all of Ma's knowledge as he watched her aging hands at work.

CHAPTER THREE

It was the start of senior year and Ma's health started to worsen, having complications from all the medication she was taking and her diabetes playing a major factor also.

They had a discussion in which Chris voiced that he wanted to drop out of high school to take care of her, but Ma' refused to entertain the idea because she wanted him to graduate.

Relenting, Christopher attended school that first week to appease Ma'. After class let out that Friday Chris made his way through the school parking lot to the Honda, wanting to hurry home to make sure Ma' had eaten and taken her medication. He decided to text Ma' that he was on his way as he shuffled between parked cars.

Jasmine was leaning up against her boyfriend's black Mustang, waiting on him to arrive. She was staring down Chris and decided it was as good a time as any to text him after going through all the trouble to get his number from his ex-girlfriend.

Her French, white-tipped, manicured nails quickly typed, "Hey, cutie, this is Jasmine. What are you doing later?" hitting send on the text as Danny walked up on her. He had watched her checking out Christopher and now that they were face-to-face she looked spooked. Seeing the screen light up on her cell, he grabbed it out of her hand.

Opening the text message it read, "Wuz up?" Danny saw that it was from Chris and quickly boiled over, tossing her phone to the concrete floor, instantly cracking the screen.

Without hesitation, Danny was at full

speed running straight at Chris. Placing the cell in his pants pocket, Chris had reached the car, stretching his hand out for the door handle.

In the blink of an eye hands had invaded his personal space as he was pushed from the back, ramming his chest into the closed door. Catching his bearings, he quickly spun around and locked eyes with an irate Danny.

All he heard was Danny say, "Why you texting my girl?"

Taking a deep breath, trying to keep his cool, Chris responded, "What you talking about?"

In that moment Danny leaned in and swung, connecting with the back left side of Christopher's jaw, right below his ear lobe. Doing no damage, Chris countered with a quick right, straight to Danny's glass chin, which made Danny fall fast like a shattered window.

The crowd that had amassed to see the fight began to hoot and holler. Chris had knocked Danny out cold, as he lay in the parking lot after falling straight back like a freshly cut oak tree in the forest.

Jasmine had made her way through the crowd and was leaning over Danny when she began to scream out as if someone was stabbing her, "He's bleeding...help, he's bleeding bad."

Staring down at Danny, Chris noticed his white t-shirt start to turn crimson red around the collar and shoulder area.

The students began to dial 9-1-1. Everything happened so fast. Panicking, Chris jumped in his car and high tailed it out of there.

Arriving home, he saw Padre Perez's white Chevy truck in the driveway. Rushing inside, he looked spooked and had Ma' and Padre asking him, "What's wrong?"

Explaining himself he could see Ma' begin to worry. Looking at Padre Perez, "I did what you told me to." I took a deep breath and tried talking. "But he hit me in the face, so I swung back. Remember, you always told me that if someone hits me in the face then I should hit them back. If he would have just punched me in the chest, I promise I would of walked away."

Without taking a breath, he continued.

"I even questioned you about the parable when Jesus says if someone strikes you on the cheek, then you should give them your other cheek also."

Padre Perez replied, "Yes, I remember what I said to you, and I meant it too. No one has the right to hit you in the face. Jesus didn't mean allow yourself to be hit literally. That parable is the same for the definition of insanity, doing the same thing over and over expecting a different result. Jesus meant if someone does you wrong and you allow the door to stay open to them, they will continue to hurt you. In essence, if they strike you on the cheek, then just give them the other cheek because it's coming. Christopher, you defended yourself and we will..."

Just then they were interrupted by a knock at the door. "Austin P.D., open up."

Ma' walked over and opened the door.

"Ma'am, we are looking for Christopher Espinosa."

"I'm his grandmother. What do you want with him?"

"Ma'am, your grandson has assaulted

a young man who was just rushed to the emergency room in an ambulance."

Frightened, he took a deep breath and approached the cops, "I'm Christopher, is Danny going to be alright?"

The sergeant reached for his cuffs, "I don't know, son, but right now you are coming with me. Now turn and place your hands behind your back."

Padre Perez got between Chris and the cops, pleading, "Christopher says it was self-defense. That the boy hit him first and he swung back. There were no weapons involved, and Chris was not the initiator here."

"Sir, we are conducting an investigation as we speak with the reports from the eyewitnesses, and we have officers looking at the video obtained from the cameras in the parking lot to see if his story matches up. If it does check out and it is truly self-defense, then he will be released into your custody, ma'am."

"Can we please be reasonable here? I'm Padre Perez, the priest at St. Peter's, 10 minutes from here. How about you conduct your investigation, and if the video and witness statements do not support Chris's story, then his grandmother and I will personally drive him to you at the station to turn himself into your custody. However, if his story does match up with all the evidence, then this can all be dropped and we can concentrate on praying for the injured young man," handing the sergeant a card from St. Peter's with his priestly picture, name, and cell number.

Taking the card, the officer replied, "Only because you're a man of the cloth, I will concede this time." Turning his gaze at Christopher, "Let's hope for your sake you are telling the truth."

Turning to exit the house, Padre thanked them as he shut the door.

Ma' looked terribly shaken, and Christopher was distraught from the ordeal. Padre guided Ma' to the couch, then he left and returned with a bottled water for Ma', motioning for Christopher to come over, "Now let's pray for this young man's healing."

Concluding the prayer and making the

sign of the cross, Christopher said to Padre Perez, "Now I know why Jesus said pray for your enemies. It's not for what they will do to you, but for what you might do to them."

Puzzled, Padre decided to not even comment. He'd rather stay focused on the happenings at the moment.

An hour later Padre's phone rang. Answering, he listened intently, then said, "Thank you," before hanging up.

Looking over at an antsy Chris, he related the message, "Your story checked out, and all charges have been dropped."

Elated, Christopher thanked God like he had never done before. Ma' sat in silence, and when Christopher saw her face he asked, "What's wrong?"

"I don't feel so good," she muttered.

At once Padre and Christopher were rushing Ma' out the door and into Padre's truck so they could rush her to the hospital.

She would later be diagnosed with the flu and would have to stay at the hospital, so Chris decided that no matter the duration of her stay, he would be by her side. Converting the wooden chair in the room into his makeshift bed, he would only leave to shower and grab something to eat.

On the third day of Ma's hospitalization Christopher took it upon himself to drop out of high school. After having caught a break with the assault charge, he more than dreaded the return. Being 18, he only needed to sign the papers, then he rushed back to Ma's side. Entering the parking lot to the hospital he was happy to see Danny walking out with his parents in tow. Christopher thanked God for Danny's healing as he got out of the car with a glowing smile plastered to his face.

It had been two weeks, and with Ma's diabetes, age, and this bout with the flu, the doctor had informed Chris that she may not recover.

That night holding Ma's hand to comfort her as they talked, Ma' told Christopher what was to be expected of him, making him promise to never do drugs, smoke, or drink alcohol. As she aptly stated, "I loved your grandfather dearly, but when he drank those spirits, I didn't like him much," infusing in him to follow his dreams and hold on tight to Jesus Christ so that his blessing will be in the form of a good woman to have a family with.

"How will I know when I've found the right one?"

"You will know because from day one you will feel as if you've known her forever."

Smiling, Chris replied, "Yes, ma'am."

Closing her eyes, "I'm going to rest now."

Kissing her gently on the forehead, "I love you, Ma'," he whispered as he settled into the chair for some sleep also.

Startled out of his sleep by the beeping sound indicating a flat line coming from the monitor, Christopher reached out for Ma's soft, aged hand. Looking up he saw the nurses flooding the room. He was quickly escorted out so that they could attend to Ma'.

Quietly, Chris sat in the waiting room with tears streaming down his baby face, knowing in his heart that he had heard Ma's enchanting voice for the last time because God had called her home.

Moments later the Spanish doctor approached him to confirm his train of thought. Now with all the family he loved gone, Christopher was feeling lost and alone in this cold, dark world.

Chapter Four

After acquiring a job at Walmart in the electronics department, Chris began to save money for what he hoped to be his future education. He wanted to live out his dream of creating a new plant species.

Ma' had left him her quaint one story, three-bedroom, red brick home along with the emerald green Honda Accord. Busy with work to save money for college, he also went to night school to obtain his GED.

The next five years would go by in a blur, having never missed Sunday Mass and his frequent talks with Padre Perez. Deciding to build a greenhouse with some of his savings, he enlisted the help of Padre Perez twice a week. The project would take six months to complete.

Growing up he was constantly told by Padre and Ma' that he would succeed. Those words were the fuel that kept him pushing forward, persevering and focused on success.

Just when he thought he would be one step closer to fulfilling his dream by being back in the classroom, the Honda began to give him problems. Not foreseeing the car breaking down and needing something reliable, he went to the nearest dealership, gave the Honda as a trade-in, and paid off the balance in cash on a brand new, silver Chevrolet Impala.

Having the setback, he now went back to square one of acquiring savings for school.

It would take years, until the age of 35, he would finally set foot on the University of Texas campus in Austin taking horticulture and business patent courses to further him along in obtaining his dream.

Christopher had sat in the local barbershop's chair for an hour allowing the pretty, young Latina, Gabby, to braid his hair into an intricate design and trim his full beard, lining it to perfection. Gabby was the best in the business, but she lacked Ma's touch, Chris thought.

Wearing a Houston Astros blue, fitted t-shirt and blue jeans with white Nike Air Max shoes as he walked into horticulture class that first day, prepared and determined to soak up the knowledge.

Surveying the room, he instantly lost focus when he laid eyes on a very attractive, petite Latina. Her long, silky, jet-black hair was reminiscent to Ma's. Glancing at her long legs wrapped in skintight, faded denim, complementing her white blouse.

From where Chris stood, she looked to be every bit of five feet seven inches, complete with a light caramel complexion, igniting his sweet tooth that had Christopher craving a butterscotch from just her looks.

Never one to be forward, he couldn't

help it as he found himself making a straight beeline to introduce himself. Taking a seat next to her, he was entranced by her enchanting hazel eyes as they talked, exchanging numbers and email addresses so they could continue to conversate during the professor's lecture under the guise of taking notes on their laptops.

Starting off with small talk, Christopher would learn her name was Angelica and she was from Dallas, also finding out that they were 10 years apart and Angelica had an older sister, Christina, well, half-sister from her father's previous marriage.

After the class had ended Christopher looked over at Angelica and asked, "Would you like to get to know each other better over coffee at Starbucks?"

"I would love to," replied Angelica in her Latina accent as she grabbed her belongings.

Enjoying the gentle, morning breeze of the two-block stroll off campus, it was during the walk to Starbucks that Angelica revealed to Chris that she had lost both of her parents to a drunk driver two years prior. Chris abruptly stopped mid-stride. Seeing her face he could feel her pain, offering his heartfelt condolences with a warm embrace to console her heart.

Standing there in that moment, Chris opened up about the loss of his parents, explaining that when Ma' passed on he felt lost in the abyss of this dark world.

Angelica threw her arms around his neck. With tears in both their eyes, they shared the same scar on their hearts. Drying his eyes, Chris then used his thumbs to wipe Angelica's supple cheeks dry. Leaning in, he kissed Angelica's soft, pink lips. In that instant, as they shared a kiss, it was as if their pain had dissipated, if only for a moment.

Taking her hand in his, they continued their walk around the corner to Starbucks.

Over lattes Angelica learned all about his past and upbringing, finding Christopher handsome, intelligent, and in love with his long hair. It was a plus that he was also Catholic. Angelica loved her faith and couldn't bear to see herself with a man that didn't share in her beliefs.

Christopher was astonished to learn that Angelica's dream was to have her own restaurant. That way she could help feed the people and the poor. Her Catholic upbringing had taught her to rely heavily on Jesus with every step she took, and that's exactly what she had done since she was a young girl.

All Christopher could help thinking was, how could she be so beautiful and so good-hearted? She made him want to be a better man just being in her presence.

From that day on they would both look forward to their time together and conversations in and out of class. Talking all night with each other was the now-daily routine.

Inviting her over to study, Angelica agreed to come only on the understanding that she could braid his hair. Giving anything to spend time with Angelica, he happily agreed. Ordering a deep dish, meat lover's from Pizza Hut that night, they ate after studying and then watched a rom-com. Angelica sat on the couch with Chris on the floor, his back to her, sitting between her legs getting his hair braided. They had the volume low enough to conversate, making

Chris's ears perk up when he heard her say she was only taking horticulture for one semester to learn how to pair up the various vegetables, spices, and peppers to enhance the seasoning, enhancing the flavors of the food.

Upon hearing that news, Christopher's mind sprung into action, comprising a plan to keep Angelica by his side.

Leaving work early the next day, Christopher went out and bought an engagement ring, using the last of his savings to purchase a stunning diamond ring.

When Angelica arrived that night to what she thought was to be a study night had her blown away by the sights and smells of filet mignon, long green beans, mashed potatoes with white gravy, served over candlelight and a bottle of chilled red wine, with smooth R&B music playing low in the background, setting the romantic ambience.

Christopher allowed her to take a sip of wine and then he wasted no time in dropping to one knee and proposing.

Three weeks later and before the

semester was over, they were married. Padre Perez presided over the small ceremony.

Angelica's older half-sister Christina had flown in to witness the union, although it seemed that as soon as the vows were said she was one foot out the door, headed to the airport to fly back to Seattle to her awaiting husband and four kids.

Christopher couldn't help but think everything was falling into place. He'd finally had someone to love again.

Staring at her handsome husband in his white tailor-made tux, Angelica hoped God would bless them with a daughter so she could pass down her white wedding dress.

✦

CHAPTER FIVE

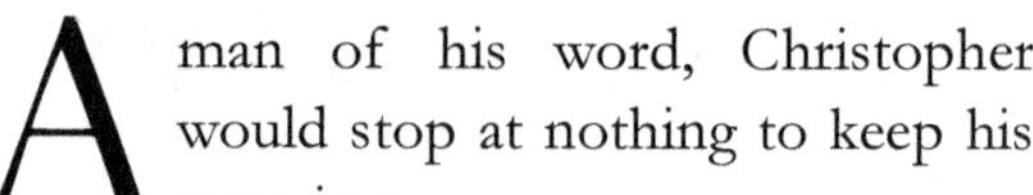

A man of his word, Christopher would stop at nothing to keep his promises.

It seemed almost instantaneous that as soon as they brought Nevaeh home, he buried himself into his work, missing out on her little life because he was diligently breeding and grafting various plants in hopes of propagating a new creation so he could stake his claim at discovery and bring his family financial stability, affording him the opportunity to keep his promise and purchase Angelica her restaurant "Ambrosia's."

Painstakingly working at Walmart during the day, then in the greenhouse on his nursery of plants and flowers during the evening, oftentimes well off into the night.

Although he would be in the next room, his makeshift home office, or outside trying to cultivate a breakthrough, he was never really there. Oftentimes Angelica felt lonely but was content and focused on raising Nevaeh, knowing in her heart her husband was doing his best to provide and take care of them.

Every third night Christopher would cut a fresh rose from the immaculate bushes planted by Ma's green thumb, the same ones he had promised to keep pruned and pristine. Placing that beautiful rose in full bloom, often a yellow one for her favorite color, in the glass vase next to her side of the bed. That way his gorgeous wife would open her eyes to love and beauty, the same way he gets to every morning he wakes up next to her.

Entering the living room on a Saturday

morning, he saw his girls sitting on the couch watching cartoons when all of a sudden Navaeh pointed at the flat screen with her chubby, half-curled index finger, and muttered out, "Booooo."

Up to this point her vocabulary had been limited to "no" and "mama." Hearing "boo" for the first time was so delightful to Chris's ears. Seeing that she was pointing at the cartoon bear Winnie the Pooh, he sought to correct her, "No, mija, it's Pooh."

In disagreement, Nevaeh exclaimed, "No…boo…booooo!"

"Okay, mija," Chris relented, "it's boo."

Angelica spoke in her sweet accent, "My love, shouldn't we teach her properly?"

"Yes, mi amor, I agree. But just this once if my princess says it's boo then I can live with that. As a matter of fact, from this day forth, mija's nickname will be Boo."

Smiling away, Nevah shook her head in agreement. Causing her pigtails to shake violently. Speaking in her childish tone, "Booo!"

"Ok, little missy, it's time to go," Angelica voiced as she stood, grabbing her purse and car keys. Picking up Nevaeh from the couch, she glanced over at Chris.

"We are going to the church to help our three favorite nuns. Sister's Benina, Olga and Paula prepare food for the homeless. Are you coming?"

"I'll be there in time to serve the food. I texted Frank and he's on the way. I want to show him some of the progress I've made. Plus I'll get him to help out also. So count on us being there in about an hour mi amor."

"Call me when you're on the way my love."

"Of course mi amor." Walking them to the door, he kissed his queen and then his princess on her forehead. Looking into Nevaeh's hazel eyes, "You be good and listen to momma, Boo."

He saw her smile, then she began to giggle as she nodded her head yes before closing the door behind them.

Ten minutes later Frank was surveying Chris's research. Frank was the same age as Angelica. Tall with a slight build, he was half-Italian and Mexican with dark brown, short hair, and a thick, black mustache. They had been friends since the University, meeting in business patenting class about four months after Christopher and Angelica's wedding. Frank had sought out to have his own firm. He was a business attorney and patent agent working out of his home office. A workaholic like Chris, they saw in each other a means to accomplishing their goals. Keen in his Christian faith, he also attended St. Peter's Catholic church.

After carefully examining the data Frank came to a conclusion. "My brother, you are certainly on course to making that breakthrough. Just remember to call me when you do so that I can take care of all the preliminaries."

Chris checked the time on his watch. "I think we should be going. We have an appointment at church to help serve the homeless. I signed you up last minute, hope you don't mind."

"Sounds like a plan," replied Frank, making his way to the front door. "Let's make a move. I'm never late for an appointment, especially in the house of the Lord."

Chapter Six

The years had flown by in the blink of an eye. Nevaeh was now six with her seventh birthday on the horizon. She was more rambunctious than ever with a heart of gold. Chris was hoping and praying more than ever for a breakthrough to come soon so he could give Boo a big birthday bash.

For the last year Christopher had made a family ritual of driving out to the prominent, luxurious estates of

Sweetwater after Sunday Mass where these breathtaking, elegant, multimillion-dollar estates were on full display. He had his heart set on a plush, extravagant, venetian-style mansion, complete with all the amenities worthy of Versailles. Resembling a cathedral, Christopher assumed that the architect honed into his Christian faith and impeccably, yet serenely, brought that vision to life.

Wanting to give his family the best the world had to offer, Chris would convey to his girls that they would live in that home one day. Boo would always be mesmerized by the sheer beauty and size of the home, inquiring about the pool and asking if she could have a puppy to play with when they moved in? Having shown her parents a picture months ago of a yorkie that she tore out of a magazine.

Chris would make mention of the pool having a grotto and how he would teach her to swim when they moved in. Falling victim to those adorable eyes, he would gladly appease her puppy request too. Boo was elated each time like she was hearing it for the very first time.

Angelica had incorporated a ritual of her own. On Sunday night after dinner, they would go into the living room to pray the rosary as a family.

Seeing his dream taking longer than anticipated, Christopher started to reminisce on the poetic words Ma' had spoken to him about how she had cared for her plants. That's when it hit him like a ton of bricks falling out of the sky. He leaped into action, jumping inside the car and driving to the corner store. Purchasing a single 32-ounce beer, he headed back home. Going through the side gate he entered the back yard knowing he had time because Angelica was preparing dinner.

Walking into the greenhouse he approached the plants. Seeing them neatly arranged and full of colorful peppers, he began to speak, "We have been in this give-and-take relationship for quite awhile. I give you water, sunlight, and care, and you give me plenty of fresh peppers. I take your peppers to eat, and you take my valuable time. Everything has been great so far, but

I need you guys to do the unimaginable and produce a pepper that is not known to man."

Opening the bottle of beer, he began to pour small amounts on the soil surrounding each plant. "I need this more than anything, and for this I will always do my part to bring you life with my two hands." Walking out of the greenhouse he poured out the rest of the beer onto the ground by the back gate then discarded the empty bottle into the trash can so no one would be the wiser.

Saying a quick prayer to God, "Please Lord, answer my prayers," then making the sign of the cross, he headed back inside to the good-smelling food Angelica was cooking.

With their bellies full and their prayer ritual concluded, Christopher snuck outside to the greenhouse to check on the nursery and maybe even converse some more with the plants.

That's when he saw a new plant amongst his jalapeno peppers. The plant had not only sprouted but was in full bloom complete with a multitude of never-before-seen red and green peppers. The plant, standing tall, smack dab in the middle of his rows, separated the Senorita and Rome jalapeno plant arrangement, surrounded by habanero pepper plants all around. Plucking the jalapeno he observed the crack-resistant, reddish-green, three-inch pepper. It was bell-shaped on top where it was red and then stretched to a point like most conventional jalapenos.

Running inside to alert the girls, he handed the jalapeno to Angelica. Scooping up Nevaeh, he rushed them outside to witness the miracle.

With the overhead light shining brightly on the singular plant, Chris looked at his wife, "Mi amor, it's a miracle. I never planted this seed. Look where it's positioned. I never plant outside of the perfectly lined rows I arranged. Feel the texture of the leaves."

Rubbing her fingers over the leaves, Angelica was full of excitement.

"How did it start growing, daddy?"

"Boo, today God has made a way and answered our prayers. He is the creator of all, and he has blessed us with this plant in our garden."

Placing his arm around his wife so he could hug them both, they basked in the blessing of the Lord.

That night he didn't get a wink of sleep until 5 a.m. Searching for an identical plant and jalapeno online, he scoured hours of data, and after finding no trace he knew without a doubt that his dream had come true.

Using the seeds from the jalapenos he planted a hundred seeds into a fresh potting bed. Feeling like his work was done, he finally fell asleep only to wake up two hours later.

First thing in the morning he called his supervisor at Walmart to inform him he was taking a sick day plus his two-week paid vacation starting tomorrow.

During breakfast Angelica kept analyzing the jalapeno Christopher had given her last night. They had talked about this moment for years and now the day had arrived. Angelica was tasked with creating a new chile hot sauce.

Seeing his wife's beautiful hazel eyes

analyze the jalapeno, he figured she needed some words of encouragement. "I know one thing for sure, it don't matter if you're brown, black, white, Asian, or Native American, everyone has a bottle of hot sauce in their kitchen."

Hearing Nevaeh giggle, Angelica replied, "I think I got it, my love."

"I know you got this, mi amor. I believe in you the same way you've believed in me all these years. I'm taking mija to the park and then to the theater to watch the new Dora the Explorer movie. We'll make it a father-daughter day. That way we're out of your hair, mi amor, and we will return with pizza for dinner."

With those last words they were out the door, leaving Angelica to accomplish the task at hand. Her mind began cycling how she could create the perfect salsa.

Steadfast in her passion for food and spice, Angelica never realized the hours that had passed, looking up to see them enter the kitchen, Christopher carrying a deep-dish meat lovers from Pizza Hut.

Greeted with a radiant smile from

Angelica, although spent, her smile gleamed triumphantly.

Walking up to his wife, Chris was met with a silver platter filled with hot wings, chips, and a bowl of salsa. Picking up a tortilla chip he scooped a nice portion of salsa. Devouring the chip, he allowed the salsa to engulf his taste buds, shooting a pleasure beat straight to his heart.

Speechless, he reached out for one of the wings saturated with Angelica's touch of spice. Taking a bite he was instantly encompassed by Mexican, Asian, and Caribbean flavors along with good ol' American texture grappling at his taste buds.

Without a second thought he exalted, "Holy shhweet Jesus!" Taking a breath, "Wow, that's hot."

All three began to laugh out loud. Chris wiped his hands clean with a napkin then immediately called Frank.

Hearing him answer, Chris said, "I need you to get over here ASAP. We finally did it, my brother."

It took 20 minutes for Frank to arrive but when he did Chris was ready, taking him straight to the kitchen where the hot wings awaited.

Pointing at the wings, "Try one of those."

After one bite Frank exclaimed, "Mmmmmm, that's good and hot." Taking another bite, then another, he continued, "The heat doesn't linger on your tongue and even vanishes slowly. Even better, it's bearable as long as you keep eating. It looks like you hit it on the nail, Chris."

"We did this together. That includes you, Frank."

"Looks like you will be needing a plant patent done, my friend."

"That's the idea, my brother. Now how much are the fees and the patent all together?"

"I will take care of all that. You have to let me do my part, Chris. First order of business is getting some pictures of the plant. Show me the way."

Heading to the greenhouse Chris escorted Frank to the miracle plant. "I have all the early data and I will know exactly how long they take to harvest from the data I will collect from the hundred more I planted last night. I've also done a thorough dig to retrieve any replicas or identical plants on the internet."

"Then we should be good. I'll get started on the plant patent first thing in the morning." Taking pictures with his phone, Frank continued, "What will you be naming the newfound jalapeno?"

"The Chriang pepper," Chris replied.

"Sounds good to me. Now one last thing, can I get some wings to go?"

"Of course, my brother, Angelica will gladly send you off with plenty."

"Although I would love to devour all of them for myself, I'm actually going to take them to a friend. I helped this guy secure a deal for his client with none other than Guillermo De Los Santos."

"De Los Santos, the owner of Wings That Sting?"

"Yeah, and I'm pretty sure if we can get him to taste these wings, we are guaranteed to get a deal."

"Wow, I didn't know you were connected like that, Frank."

"What can I say? I'm half Italian, I know

a guy, aye."

"As long as you don't offer me a deal I can't refuse, we're good."

Both of them laughed up a storm as they headed back inside. Chris explained to Angelica how Frank needed wings to facilitate an appointment with De Los Santos to make a business transaction transpire.

Those words had Angelica happily preparing more wings, sending Frank off with a few dozen in her best Tupperware.

CHAPTER SEVEN

In three short months Angelica's recipe was copy written and the plant patent for the Chriang pepper was pending. Christopher had successfully cultivated a hundred more plants in the greenhouse, meticulously storing all the data, learning it took exactly 73 days for the jalapenos to be ready for harvest. The miniature bell tops would start out yellow then turn reddish-green when ripe. He'd planted more seeds in preparation of 300 more plants.

It was Saturday morning, Angelica was tying her shoe as she spoke to Chris, "You've been missing in action with your volunteer work. Will you be showing up today to help with feeding the homeless?"

"Of course, mi amor, I will be showing up with Frank also, he's on his way. He said he has some good news to share."

"Good, we can use all the hands we can get. We have been having huge turnouts lately. Thank God for the many volunteers that we have."

"It's because your food is so good, sweetheart. Trust me, I would live in the streets for a week to get a plate of your brisket enchiladas."

"You're silly, my love."

"The silly part is I'm serious," replied Chris.

"Well, let me bring you up to speed with the extra volunteers that will be there. First off, Jason and Heather will be there with their two young sons. Also, Deacon Jason and wife Sandy with their three sons, Icem, Gabe, Josh, and their precious baby girl Ellie. Nevaeh and Ellie have become the best of friends. Wait until you see how cute they are together."

"Wow, that's a lot of names to remember."

"I'm just getting started, my love, there's three Johns with their wives that will be helping out. You have Deacon John and wife China with their daughter Erica and her husband Eric along with their three kids. You will recall Erica from the commercial on TV for the Crest whitening toothpaste and strips."

"I'm guessing she'll have the whitest teeth in the room."

"Then there's brother John with wife Amy and their children Jayden and Janie. Last, but not least, brother John, his wife Wendy, and their daughter."

"All these Johns remind me of the Reyes brothers. They were all named Jesús. We had to call them Big Jesús, Little Jesús, and Baby Jesús to differentiate between the three, but everyone knew their mother loved her some Jesus."

"Brother Ed will also be there with his wife…," stopping midsentence as she saw smoke practically coming out of his ears from the overload of information he was amassing in such a short time.

"How about I just give you a head's up by whispering in your ear as we get ready to make contact with the volunteers?"

"Mi amor, you make me look good, in more ways than one."

"Yes, I do," replied Angelica with a wink, taking Naveah by the hand as they walked out the front door.

When Frank arrived, he was ecstatic. "We got the patent and a meeting with De Los Santos on Wednesday. Jerry, the guy I told you I worked with, got the dozen wings I gave to him to De Los Santos. The man loved them, and he wants to make a deal. He'll be in town to oversee the progress of his forthcoming Wings That Sting grand opening in two months."

"This is a dream come true. Let's discuss our plan of action for the upcoming meeting on our way to church. Angelica needs our help this morning to help feed the homeless."

"Sure thing," replied Frank as they walked out the door.

❖   ❖   ❖

Padre Perez gave a heartfelt homily at Mass, his words still resonating with Chris as he drove through Sweetwater per their Sunday morning ritual. Seeing the splendor of the estates it dawned on Christopher what seemed more than ever a possible reality to own their dream home.

Pulling up to the venetian-style mansion, he was in instant shock to see that the estate was for sale. Grabbing his cell, he quickly entered the name, Tanisha Guillory, and number that was displayed next to a picture of a pretty, young, black woman on the realtor's sign.

"Daddy, what does that sign mean?"

"It means everything seems to be falling in place, Boo."

"So can we move in for my seventh birthday on Saturday?" Without taking a breath she continued, "And can I have my puppy for my present?"

"I certainly hope so," replied Chris, squeezing Angelica's hand as he drove off.

During his lunch hour at work on Monday he called the realtor.

"Hello, this is Tanisha speaking."

"Hello, my name is Christopher."

"Hi, Christopher. How can I help you?"

"I'm calling about the venetian-style mansion in Sweetwater that's for sale."

"Yes sir, it has been on the market for four short days, and I already have two potential buyers, so you may want to act fast. The asking price is at a firm 22 million. It comes fully furnished, also. The sprawling 18,717 square foot mansion is five years old and comes with eight bedrooms, 10 full bathrooms, a spacious master bedroom with fireplace, plus an exquisite master bath. It comes complete with a theater, gym, spa, and a heated 60,000-gallon pool with grotto by the fire pit. The amenities include an indoor basketball court and a 20-car garage amid the home's meticulously kept 72,000 square foot lush landscape, not to mention vaulted ceilings and two elevators.

"Sounds amazing, Tanisha."

"So, would you like to schedule a walkthrough, Christopher?"

"No need, ma'am. This is the home I want for my family. I only have one slight problem. I would need you to stall any potential clients until Wednesday. I have an important meeting on Wednesday morning at 10 a.m. If all goes as planned, I will have purchased the home from you by noon. Also, I would be willing to compensate you for your troubles."

Hearing him out, Tanisha replied, "Sir, with Wednesday being right around the corner, I think I may be able to stall for you, but only till noon."

"Thank you, Tanisha, you're a blessing. I will have my attorney Frank call you and make the transaction Wednesday morning should the business deal go according to plan."

"Good luck on your deal, sir."

"Thank you, ma'am."

Ending the call, Christopher crossed himself, silently thanking God for the many blessings.

Before leaving work that day Christopher met with his supervisor to give his two-week notice.

CHAPTER EIGHT

⟐

Straightening Christopher's light blue tie and checking the design she spent over an hour braiding, Angelica looked into her husband's eyes, "You got this, my love. All the hard work is done. This is the easy part." Dressed to impress with his nicely trimmed goatee, he leaned in and kissed his wife. Christopher then grabbed his black suit jacket off the bed.

"I'm taking mija to the dentist for a check-up at 9:30 a.m. Then we will head over to church to light a candle for you and pray the rosary."

Throwing on his suit jacket, he entered the living room to an awaiting Frank in his black business suit. Holding a clear Tupperware container with a dozen wings inside and a 5" by 7" index card containing Angelica's recipe with the other hand.

"Time to go, brother. Follow me in your car," Frank said.

"Let's hope everything works out."

"High hopes, daddy," Nevaeh chimed in in her innocent voice.

"Good luck, my love," Angelica said in her Latin accent as they left out the door.

Exiting the dentist's office, Nevaeh was adjusting her new Wonder Woman ring back and forth on her little finger. It was a gift for having such clean teeth. Angelica was glad to see Nevaeh proudly sporting her gold plastic ring and the visit going so well because she knew how much Nevaeh dreaded going to the dentist.

Approaching the car, "Now, let's go to church so we can pray for daddy."

Entering the meeting, Christopher knew

to just let Frank do most of the talking and try to keep a straight face when the negotiations started. Frank had mentioned the amount of money he was looking to acquire. The number had left Christopher dumbfounded, and he knew he would have to keep his mind focused on the girls in order to refrain from accepting the first number being offered.

After the greetings it was down to business. Mr. De Los Santos had previously eaten a few of the wings he was presented with when they first arrived.

With everyone seated at the huge mahogany table and De Los Santos sitting at the head in his expensive, pristine, dark blue suit, overlooking each other as they all wore their game faces, De Los Santos gave a slight nod to his lawyer positioned at his right hand.

The older, white-haired gentleman wearing gold wire-rim glasses and a black business suit began to state, "Hello, gentlemen. My name is Tom and I'm Mr. De Los Santos' business attorney."

Christopher shifted in his seat to get

comfortable as he and De Los Santos prepared to be entertained by their lawyers' negotiation chops.

"Mr. De Los Santos is prepared to buy the exclusive rights to the recipe today for the price of 100 million with the guarantee that you will be able to sustain the demand of the Chriang peppers at $1.75 a pound."

Frank countered, "I've done my research, Tom, and the Wings That Sting franchise is currently at 150 locations in 40 states, with a projected expansion of a dozen more locations in the next three years. Going over the numbers just during football season generates well over a million for each location, every franchise bringing in revenue of over four million annually. So, walking out of here with a $100 million check is certainly not to our benefit. My client proposes the purchase of the rights to the recipe for 300 million and the supply of his patented Chriang peppers through the Chriang LLC for the cost of $2 a pound."

"Although we can come to an agreement for $2 a pound for the Chriang peppers, the 300 million asking price is very steep. While the revenue encumbered by each location may be true, you fail to account for the expenses for running the business and the thousands of employees."

Chris was still working on controlling his breathing and body to keep from jumping out of the chair upon hearing Frank counter with 300 million. Surveying the faces on everyone, it was apparent the negotiations were just about to heat up.

❖   ❖   ❖

Greeted by Padre Perez, who was leaving the church to get coffee and doughnuts, he had told Angelica he would return shortly with plenty for them also and a chocolate milk for Nevaeh. Excited about her plastic gold ring with red Wonder Woman symbol protruding from the top, she made it a point to flash the ring at Padre before he left their sight.

Lighting a small white candle, Angelica and Nevaeh were holding their rosaries, about to begin praying, when Deacon Albert approached them.

"It's nice to see you two this morning. I hope the music doesn't bother you. I can turn it down if you'd like."

"No need, Deacon, we actually are enjoying it. It's not every day you hear a choir singing in Latin."

"That's the Bonaventure choir of nuns singing. I believe the Latin captures the nostalgia of the Catholic faith."

"Yes, it truly does, Deacon."

Deacon Albert shut the thick wooden doors to the chapel, allowing the sweet harmony to echo in God's house as "Ave Maria" began to play.

Walking up the few steps to the entrance of the church was a short, pale, chubby man with a pock-marked face, his scraggly beard trying to cover the craters. In his late 20s, he was already going bald from all the years of stress. Entering St. Peter's, he saw the thick, wooden, double doors closed and heard the choir singing. He automatically thought the church was full of people. Making a sharp right, he went into the men's restroom and placed the black backpack he was carrying into the trashcan. Taking the black cell phone with the 10-digit code displayed across the screen, he stuck it in the back pocket of his pants, then rushing out to his car a block away to retrieve another backpack, wanting to have as many casualties as possible.

The tranquility that infused their souls as they heard the choir of angelic voices sing "Ave Maria" was so enlightening, Deacon Albert had joined in on praying the rosary. Nevaeh began to recite the prayers, jubilated that she had finally learned to pray them by heart. Secretly, she couldn't wait to show her father on Sunday night.

Making the trek back to his car had Abdul-Akbar Hasan huffing and puffing for air by the time he made it. Reaching into the back seat to grab the red backpack full of explosives and the red phone that was the detonator, he happened to bend over just enough to have his backside hit the send button on the screen, detonating the bomb already planted inside the church.

Holding the red backpack and phone in his hands, the power from the blast blew out all the windows and slammed the door on the car, tossing him like a tumbleweed in a sandstorm 10 feet onto the sidewalk.

Knocked unconscious, he laid there amongst the piercing sounds of car alarms and terrified screams from the onlookers. The car was still rocking back and forth as people began to look in his direction.

❖   ❖   ❖

With a nod of the head from De Los Santos, Tom continued. "Although my client felt that 100 million was more than fair, he is willing to pay out 180 million."

Without flinching, Frank stated, "Mr. De Los Santos is having a grand opening in a few months. What's grander than opening a new location with the unveiling of a new flavor of hot wings? We strongly feel that the profit margin for Wings That Sting will increase more than 40 percent in its first year of adding this new flavor. For that reason, my client is comfortable selling for 250 million."

Tom glanced at Mr. De Los Santos,

who waved him off, then spoke directly to Christopher in an assertive tone, "210 million is my final offer."

Without hesitancy, "Deal," replied Christopher.

"Good," De Los Santos said, as he rose to his feet to shake Frank and Christopher's hands. "Glad we could make a deal today, gentlemen."

"Likewise, sir," Chris said with a smile.

"Tom, have the money transferred within the next 10 minutes," De Los Santos instructed as Christopher signed the dotted line on the contract before him. After the signature was inked, De Los Santos retrieved the recipe on the 5" by 7" index card, then exited the room before it could dry.

Christopher conveyed to Tom he wanted 160 million deposited into his account and the other 50 million to be placed in Frank's account.

"I'll have the transfers done in the next 10 minutes, sir."

"50 million," Frank exclaimed.

"I need you to purchase the home from Tanisha for me for 22 million and bless her with 1 million for her troubles. The rest is for you. Now you'll have the practice that you always dreamed about."

"Thank you, bro. I'll have the home purchased for you in the next 30 minutes."

Looking at his watch, "That's perfect timing," thinking that left 20 minutes to spare.

Walking out of the office building, Christopher couldn't believe what had just taken place. Before starting his car, he breathed out a sigh of relief. Then the excitement hit him. As he put the key in the ignition, he couldn't wait to get home and tell his family to pack because they were moving tomorrow morning.

CHAPTER NINE

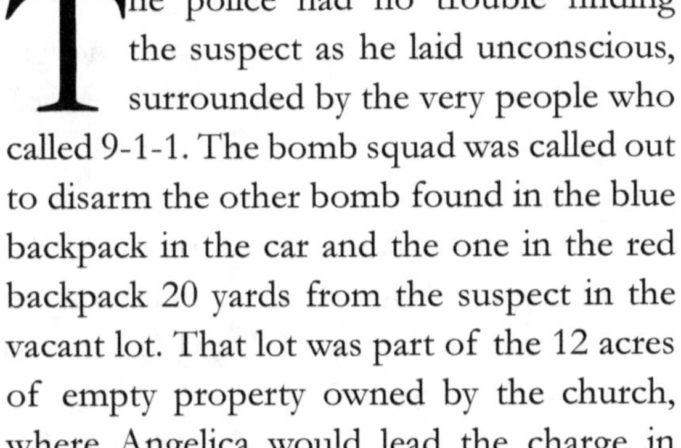

The police had no trouble finding the suspect as he laid unconscious, surrounded by the very people who called 9-1-1. The bomb squad was called out to disarm the other bomb found in the blue backpack in the car and the one in the red backpack 20 yards from the suspect in the vacant lot. That lot was part of the 12 acres of empty property owned by the church, where Angelica would lead the charge in feeding the homeless every Saturday.

Abdul-Akbar Hasan was cuffed and sitting in a small, cold room. The interrogation process was about to begin, and the detectives wanted answers.

Overcome with excitement, Christopher could barely make out what Tanisha was saying.

"Tanisha, you're going to have to slow down so I can understand what you're saying."

"Oh my God, Christopher, really, you gave me a million dollars?"

Hearing the tears in her voice, "I think everyone at one time or another has prayed for a million dollars. Consider this your prayer answered."

"Christopher, I can't thank you enough. You have no idea what you've done for me."

"Just take care of yourself and your family and we're even."

"Yes, sir, oh, and before I forget, the home is yours. You can move in tomorrow. I gave Frank two sets of keys. Thank you again for the blessing."

"It was my pleasure," Christopher replied, ending the call.

Pulling into his driveway, he saw Padre Perez leaning up against his truck. With no sign of Angelica's car, thoughts began to run around in his mind. Since her phone kept going straight to voicemail, he summed it up as her still being at church volunteering, as usual.

Approaching Padre, Chris was close enough to see the tears flowing from his bloodshot eyes. That's when his heart hit the floor. Unable to take another step, frozen in time because he knew something was terribly wrong.

Padre Perez stood in front of him and through muffled speech said, "They're all in heaven now, Christopher." Padre quickly placed his arms around him as his legs began to wane and his knees buckled. Hearing those words brought fire to his chest.

"How? What do you mean, Padre? What happened?"

Holding him up with a bear hug, Padre spoke softly into his ear. "A bomb blew up the church and everyone inside. Deacon Albert, Angelica, and Nevaeh are with God now, Christopher."

Knowing Padre wouldn't lie to him, he couldn't comprehend how this could be the truth.

Regaining his legs back, he pulled away from Padre. "Let's go to the church. I have to go…"

"No, Christopher, there's nothing left. Let's go inside and you can watch the news."

Feeling numbness throughout his body, Chris still managed to make it to the living room, turning on the TV to CNN, enhancing the volume to hear the news anchor clearly, "If you've just joined us, we are covering a suspected terrorist bombing at St. Peter's Catholic Church in Austin, Texas, with three confirmed dead and the suspected bomber in custody. The suspect is a 28-year-old Syrian immigrant with ties to an extremist group formed in Iraq. The FBI have reported Abdul-Akbar Hasan showed an online history of terrorist militia at rallies chanting, "Death to Zion."

Christopher wanted to throw up at the sight of his ugly mug plastered on the screen.

The news anchor continued, "He had

immigrated to America at the age of four and for the past year has invested countless hours watching extremist propaganda from the Islamic state. For the last two months he has watched videos on how to make bombs with C4, a highly potent explosive. The FBI has also confirmed that it was through the black market that he was able to obtain the explosives, with three people dead and the youngest reported at five years old."

"She was six," mumbling through pouring tears. "She turned seven is three days." Chris was distraught, hitting the power button on the remote.

"How could God allow this to happen to them, Padre, in his house? Weren't they supposed to be safe in his house?"

"All three became martyrs this morning. We don't believe in coincidences. We believe in providence. So, God's will was carried out. My son, we do not question God's actions, only our own."

Filled with immense pain, they both sat in silence, staring blankly into space with uncontrollable tears pouring out of their aching hearts.

CHAPTER TEN

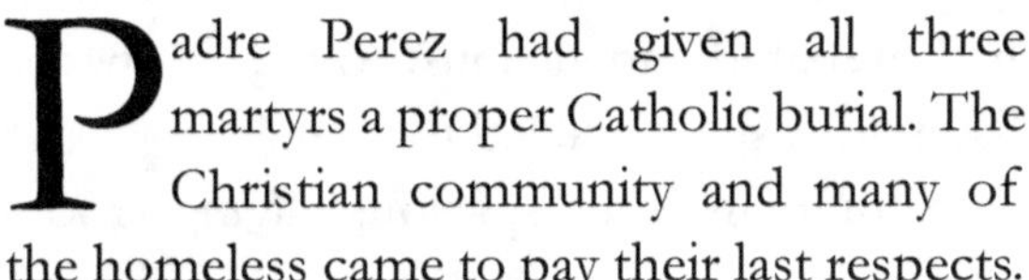

Padre Perez had given all three martyrs a proper Catholic burial. The Christian community and many of the homeless came to pay their last respects.

Christopher, dressed in all black, had shaved his face clean and cut his long hair off to the style he once wore in high school, vowing to never have long hair again because there would never be another woman in his life to braid it.

Watching as his wife's and daughter's silver urns were placed into the burial plot next to grandpa and Ma' and alongside his parents brought Christopher to a shuddering cry. The color of his suit matched the gaping hole in his heart.

In no mood for conversation, he only shared a few choice words with Frank and Christina before she left to catch a flight back home. He'd offered to pay to have the whole family flown in, but Christina politely declined and instead came alone on her own dime.

Padre drove him home to his sprawling mansion to make sure he would eat some of the food many of the women from church had prepared and also just to talk or maybe listen in case he needed to vent.

Sitting in the spacious living room surrounded by ornate décor, the reality of losing his family started to set in. Stirring up his anger, he began to breathe harder with shorter bursts of air flaring up his nostrils. Tears rolled down his cheeks and his head hung low as he glanced at Padre.

"What now? How am I supposed to live now?"

"Christopher, you must go on. We must

go on to finish out our calling."

"This guy robbed me of my life, of my heart. I'm just supposed to accept that, like nothing?"

"No, I'm not saying that. We don't ever forget, but we must continue on our Christian path."

"Honestly, Padre, I can't forgive this guy for what he did. I want to hurt him so badly. With all the money I have, I know I can have him killed in prison. An eye for an eye. I know guys from the neighborhood who are locked up who would love to have the kind of money I'm willing to offer."

Padre sat up straight and spoke sternly, "Christopher, need I remind you, you are a Godly man, and this home has been blessed, so you are on holy ground. I know that you are angry, but you must never follow through with this malicious talk. I assure you Angelica and Nevaeh are in heaven right now listening to you speak. You must continue to make them smile as you always have."

Looking intently into Christopher's eyes, Padre continued, "It is up to us to live out our lives as God-fearing men so that we may spend eternity with our loved ones. If you truly love and miss them, then you have the opportunity to be with them in the Kingdom. No more pain or suffering, only heavenly bliss. But you must do your part and live up to your calling."

Still trying to make sense of the situation, Chris nodded, "I know, Padre, it's just hard."

"Well, my son, it's not meant to be easy. Your parents named you Christopher. Christ is in your name, therefore, Christ is in you. Remember, Christ sweat blood the day before he was crucified. He knew what he must face, and he still did his part for humanity. Now that's unconditional love. I only ask you, my son, to do your part, and your reward will be eternal life with everyone you love."

Noticing he was penetrating Christopher's thought process, Padre continued to speak sensibly. "The proof is in the pudding, as they say. Look at the miracles that transpired that fateful day. Neither the Holy Eucharists on the alter nor the crucifix were harmed during the explosion although everything else was demolished. Amid all the rubble, the firefighters found their rosaries in pristine condition. Bishop Ferias wants them enshrined at the new church. And the one that blew everyone's mind was when all the onlookers, police, and firefighters heard the choir singing "Ave Maria" in Latin for 33 seconds, noticing that only one speaker was recovered in somewhat operational form, it was found out not to be connected because the CD player was obliterated. There was a handful of nonbelievers in the crowd that day. Today, those same people are praying to Jesus."

Wiping away his tears, a smile began to appear on Christopher's face.

"God is always with us, my son. Even in the midst of that horrific tragedy, God revealed himself to us. Divine providence is the belief that God is in control. Everything happens for a reason, Christopher. The only thing we can control is our faith. That's why we are called to pray without ceasing, so we are close to God. Regardless of how hard it may seem we must press on knowing He is with us every step of the way."

"Thank you for those words, Padre, I needed that. I do want to keep my promises I made to them and live out our dreams until we reunite. I saw Angelica holding Nevaeh and they were both smiling at me last night in my dream. When I awoke, I realized what I must do. Padre, I do need a favor from you."

"How can I help?"

"Could you please call Bishop Ferias to inform him that I'll be donating the money to rebuild the church, also to relate to the Vatican that I would like to purchase the 12 acres adjacent to the church. I want to construct apartment buildings to house single mothers and widows, along with a full-fledged restaurant in honor of Angelica to feed the homeless every weekend. The complex will stand on integrity and charity."

"I'll get on the phone as soon as I get home. There's one last thing I wanted to share with you before I go." Reaching into his pocket he retrieved a plastic golden ring with a red Wonder Woman symbol on top. "This is what Nevaeh was wearing that morning when I saw them. When I walked over what used to be the church, it lit up, bright and shiny in the sunlight. I just thought you might like to have it."

Trying to form words amid his gasp for air, "Thank you, Padre. You have no idea how much this means to me."

CHAPTER ELEVEN

Ten months later and construction was still underway. Chris had donated the money to rebuild the church, and the Vatican had also donated the 12 acres to Chris with an agreement the property would be used for charitable purposes exclusively housing single mothers, widows, and feeding the homeless.

The first order of business was having five massive greenhouses built on two acres to cultivate the high demand of

Chriang peppers for the Wings That Sting franchises. Frank, Padre, and plenty of church volunteers would help Chris with harvesting and packaging before he would ship them out. Having 50,000 plants needing harvesting every 73 days, Chris was so grateful to the volunteers for helping the great cause of facilitating the platform for the charity work about to unfold.

A few months shy of the timeline for the church, apartments, and restaurant set to be ready, Christopher only had one other thing lingering on his mind. The upcoming sentencing phase for Abdul-Akbar Hasan.

Knowing the prosecutor was seeking the death penalty by way of lethal injection, Padre and Chris had talked at length about going to speak as victims and also ask the judge to sentence him to life in prison.

The hearing was in the morning, and Christopher spent all night in his spacious office perfecting his victim statement, often taking a deep breath and a pause as thoughts filled his mind. How he wished to hear the girls' sweet voices and laughter reverberating throughout this great big house.

Waking up this day to face the man that had wreaked havoc on his life was something he would of liked to have missed out on, but hoping it might bring about some type of closure had him standing before Padre and Frank in his living room. Wearing the same black suit he'd worn to the funeral had him feeling empowered with the sense that the girls were with him.

Frank had driven, allowing Padre Perez and Christopher to go over their speeches. Before exiting the vehicle, they said a prayer together that would carry them into the courtroom in good spirits.

It wasn't until Christopher sat down and saw the short, fat murderer sitting in between his two lawyers wearing a black kufi covering his balding scalp and scraggly beard trying to conceal his deeply pock-marked face that his spirit became unsettled.

Padre was giving his speech, but all Chris heard was noise. He couldn't make out a word of it because he was locked in, wondering if he could burn a hole in him from staring so long. One thing for certain, if looks could kill there would be no reason for the sentencing because Abdul-Akbar would have dropped dead instantly when Chris took his seat.

The world began to slow down, and Chris's heart felt like it was being torn to pieces all over again. Catching himself, he started taking deep breaths and centering his mind in Christ instead of what was before him, helping him bounce back to reality.

Hearing his name called, he rose and approached the podium, only steps away from evil.

Beginning, he addressed the court then went into his victim impact statement. "Your honor, this man has caused irreputable damage. What he has taken from me, no one can replace. It is only by my faith and belief in Jesus that has gotten me this far. Now, today, oddly enough, I ask you to take into consideration this man's life. For the crimes he has committed he should be given a life sentence, locked away to never harm an innocent human being ever again. To give him a death sentence would be no better than what was given to my loved ones."

Standing strong, Christopher spoke

sternly, "A wise priest once told me the good die young. And your honor, my wife and daughter were good through and through." Fighting back tears, he continued, "That same priest also said you can't kill bad grass." Looking over and making eye contact, he pointed at Abdul-Akbar Hasan. "And your honor, this is the epitome of bad grass."

Turning back to face the judge, he resumed, "But nevertheless, if this man should choose to repent then maybe his soul will be spared on the day of judgment. So, for that reason, I do not wish to play God and kill this man. Instead, I ask that he be given a life sentence and face his maker in due time. Thank you, your honor."

Taking a deep breath, Chris then turned to return to his seat. Hearing a sniffling laugh followed by, "Repent for what?" Chris then abruptly focused in on his family's murderer.

In the blink of an eye, Christopher had reached him as he rose to his feet wearing cuffs and shackles around his ankles, in between his lawyers. The fire burning in Christopher's chest was unleashed as Abdul-Akbar's head jarred hard to his left after being struck with two punches in quick succession, one to the right side of his face, and the other catching his cheek and the ridge of his nose.

Leaning forward, Abdul-Akbar tried to shield his face, but instead opened himself up for Christopher, who threw a strong right uppercut straight to his mouth, making a clean connection, knocking out his top two front teeth.

Abdul-Akbar's neck snapped back, and his face grimaced in pain as he fell to the floor. The big, country-fed bailiff wrestled Christopher down. Seeing Abdul-Akbar's bloody tooth on the floor next to his hand, he snatched it up and placed it in his suit pocket right before more policemen were on his back. Giving no resistance to the bailiff and the other authorities, Christopher was quickly subdued and rushed out of the courtroom.

"Order, order in the court," Judge Garza proclaimed.

With the drama played out and Judge

Garza taking control of her courtroom through her feisty Latina attitude. While Abdul-Akbar was taken to an adjacent room to be looked at by medical staff, Frank asked to speak with the judge.

Allowing him to approach the bench, she listened to Frank convey the fact that Christopher was provoked. Judge Garza agreed that Christopher had been provoked. She had seen Abdul-Akbar say something in his direction before laughing, which she believed is what set off Chris's trigger, but she was adamant in her stance that those were still not justifiable causes for his actions.

Looking down her angular nose at Frank, she stated, "I will not hold him in contempt of court, but he must leave the premises now, meaning he cannot remain here to hear the sentencing verdict." Seeing the bailiff return she instructed him to release Chris and make sure he exited the building.

Thankful, Frank rushed out of the courtroom with Chris and Padre in tow racing for the car.

Arriving at the venetian mansion, Padre

and Frank settled into the living room to watch CNN and hear the outcome of the sentencing phase. Christopher went into the kitchen where he removed the tooth from his pocket and proceeded to clean it with Dawn dishwashing soap and warm water.

The TV was blasting, so he heard the commentator say that Abdul-Akbar Hasan was sentenced to life in prison with no possibility of parole after Judge Garza took the victim impact statements into consideration and having overlooked the outburst in the courtroom earlier this morning.

Drying off the tooth, he placed it in his pants pocket, entering the living room with a grin, "So, he got life."

"Yeah, see what he does with it," replied Frank. Grabbing his keys, "I'm heading out. I've had enough excitement for one day. I'll see y'all later," he said, walking out the front door.

Striking down Christopher with his eyes, Padre addressed the elephant in the room. "So, what happened today?"

"I don't know, Padre, I lost my temper."

"Yeah, you sure did and that surprised me."

"I'm sorry, Padre, just seeing him not remorseful and laughing in my face pushed me over the edge. I saw black…"

"Then red from his blood," Padre interjected. "I have to admit that was a clean uppercut. But Christopher, you have to control your actions no matter even if you're provoked."

Taking a deep breath, Padre continued. "Everyone's actions have ripple effects in the pool of life. That's why Jesus says He gives us living water. Yes, for eternal life to never thirst again spiritually, but also one life is as vast as the ocean. That living water transcends our paths, embodying our everyday actions. The more you continue to live a certain lifestyle, the ripples from that behavior will be cast out into the world. If you exert love every day, then love will have a resounding effect that will ripple throughout the world. Now, if you cast out stones of hate upon the water of life, then the flow of evil will have a never-ending tide that will eventually turn into a tsunami of wickedness left in the wake of people's lives."

Listening intently, Christopher hung onto Padre's every word.

"Many choose to cast stones of evil that settle into the bottom of the living water, burying themselves into the earth. That's why this world is so wicked. It is up to us to change the current, allowing love to cascade over those evil stones, eroding the sand away, only to pluck it out of existence. Remember, 71 percent of earth is water causing those evil stones to become prevalent."

"I certainly want to do my part, Padre."

"You are on the right track, Christopher, you just can't let yourself be taken off course. Allow Jesus to order your steps in righteousness. Seeing Jesus walk on water had Peter step out of the boat and walk on water towards him. It wasn't until Peter's faith wavered that he began to sink. Believe whole-heartedly that if you live out God's will for your life then you will be with your family in the Kingdom for eternity and so shall it be."

Seeking a deeper understanding of what

happened to his family, Christopher asked, "Padre, how is it that someone can become a terrorist from reading the Quran?"

"It all stems from perception and influence. I studied the Quran during seminary, and it is a beautiful text. I was astonished to learn that the blessed Virgin Mary had her own book, accurately called the Sura of Maryam. A person's perception into the interpretation may become eschewed if heavily influenced by propaganda with an ulterior motive."

Seeing Christopher wasn't quite grasping the concept, Padre decided to give a more detailed breakdown.

"Perceptions of interpretations change all across the board in religious views. Take a look at Christianity as a whole. Catholic, Orthodox, and Protestants are all Christian brethren who worship the same God. We only worship differently through our perception of interpretation of holy scripture.

"One example being the 'Our Father Prayer,' we end at, 'Deliver us from evil… Amen.' The Protestants continue with,

"For thy is the Kingdom, Power, and Glory Forever and Ever…Amen.' When the disciples asked Jesus how to pray, he replied with this prayer. Not one time in the Gospel did Jesus add the extra line. Although it is true and proper praise to God, we don't add it to the end of our 'Our Father Prayer.' Instead, we recite 'For thy is the Kingdom, Power, and Glory, Forever and Ever,' during the procession of Mass every day in praise of our Father."

"Why would they add to the perfect prayer when the last page of the Bible says don't add or take from, for this is God's word?"

"Quite simply because they needed their own identity. Just as the Orthodox church chose to remove a few choice words from the creed and proceed to cross themselves right to left instead of left to right as Catholics do. Well, that's certainly enough insight for one day. I'm going to head home."

Opening the front door for Padre, Christopher shook his hand. "Thank you for giving me clarity, Padre."

"Sure thing, Christopher, and remember,

walk on water, my son."

Closing the door behind Padre he headed upstairs to his room adorned with the family photos he had brought from Ma's house. Taking the tooth from his pocket, he put it into a small, blue velvet bag, tying the drawstrings, and placed it on the nightstand next to his side of the bed.

CHAPTER TWELVE

The day had finally arrived. The door would be opening this morning to receiving new tenants at the High Hopes Apartment Complex.

Christopher was still riding high from yesterday's first Mass at the newly rebuilt St. Peter's Catholic Church, which seated 450 comfortably. Entering the church, he was met with the smell of sweet pomegranate incense burning along with votive candles, making the long wait well worth it.

Bishop Ferias had presided over Mass along with Padre Perez with the new addition, Deacon Bob, helping out. Deacon Bob, a tall, slender, olive-skinned, humble man with short, salt and pepper hair was recently a widower and came to take on the post of Deacon a few months prior. He had a great fervor for the Lord, which was manifest in his joyful singing.

After Mass, Bishop and Padre took care in blessing the property in preparation for today, while Deacon Bob and Christopher went over plans for the influx of people.

The other 10 acres adjacent to the massive greenhouses had three stories of apartments containing two bedrooms with all new appliances including washer and dryer on the left-hand side. Seven rows of baby blue with white trim apartments along the front and five rows going horizontal. The right side of apartments consisted of three bedrooms and the whole complex was solar powered from the multiple solar panels on the roofs. The apartments were handicapped accessible to wheelchairs on the bottom floor, having the front office and Angelica's Taste of Heaven Restaurant, which seated 100 patrons, separating the two complexes. A swimming pool was also behind each apartment building with a classroom separating them. The restaurant would not only feed the tenants but also the homeless every weekend. Behind the huge classroom and adjacent daycare was a gym with treadmills and stationary bikes lined up against the far wall and elliptical machines in the center of the room. A few flat screens to keep the guests entertained, as well.

Unlocking the front door, Chris could see through the glass that there was certainly a long line of women and children. He funneled as many as he could inside, then he proceeded with the tenant process.

First up was Lola, a short Latina in her mid-30s and a single mother of three. Her youngest was tugging at her pants leg while Chris surveyed her tired eyes.

"Sir, how much for a one bedroom?"

Christopher conveyed a caring look at Lola, knowing she was in need of a break. "I see you have three children with the oldest possibly 10. I believe you will be needing more than a single bedroom. First off, do you have employment?"

"Yes, sir, I work as a waitress at Denny's, but I only make minimum wage plus tips. So, I don't think I could afford more than a one bedroom, if that. We've been staying with my mother for the past year, and I have a little saved up but not much."

"After your shift would you be willing to help out a little here in the restaurant?"

"I wouldn't mind. I mean, I'm a Christian too, well, at least I try to be. I would gladly help out in any way that I could."

"Then it's settled, you are the new tenant of a three bedroom apartment. Your rent will be the total sum of $40 a month, $33 for rent and $7 for water."

"Forty dollars a month," she blurted out in disbelief, alarming everyone in the room to the price of rent. "You must be kidding."

"No, ma'am, I'm serious as a heart attack. Now remember, you gave me your word that you would help out in the restaurant from time to time. Also, there is one catch—I implore you to pray every day, whether it be one or a hundred prayers a day."

"That's no problem, sir." Knowing his story from the highly publicized bombing of the nearby church, she continued, "But I'm not a Catholic, I'm a Protestant, raised in a Presbyterian church."

"That doesn't matter. What does is that you have a personal relationship with God. You should also know that Deacon Bob will be on hand to shuttle you to work and pick you up if need be. Also, there is zero tolerance for illegal drugs or alcohol on the premises. If found in your possession you will be immediately evicted."

"I have no problem meeting the requirements. I don't know how to thank you for this miracle you have given to my family."

"Think of it more as a blessing that you can take advantage of by positioning yourself to save money, eventually purchasing a home for your family."

Sliding the form before her, "This contract is binding for one year. After that year we will revisit your situation and go from there. One last thing, all meals are free for the first month. After that you will be required to pay a dollar for each meal. Only the kids eat free during your entire stay. Know that the complex is entirely solar powered and you have free cable."

Handing her a black ballpoint pen he pointed at the dotted line on the contract, "Sign here."

Looking at the blurred dotted line through tears of joy, she signed and was then handed the keys to her new three-bedroom apartment.

Next up was a young Asian woman with a set of twin boys recently widowed from her husband suffering from a bout of PTSD after returning home from the military. He had decided to commit suicide on what was to be their seven-year anniversary. No longer able to afford the rent on their spacious condo and also not wanting to raise the boys in the place attached to that gruesome memory, she was now before Christopher only hoping to receive a blessing like the woman before her.

"Hello, I'm Yuki and these are my five-year-old twins. I am a recent widow and I applied at the Walmart a week ago, so I'm hoping to have a job there soon. I do have some savings, though, and I'd like to know the cost of a one bedroom?"

"Yuki, I'm Christopher." Taking a deep breath, he looked at Yuki with kind eyes. "My condolences for your loss."

"Thank you, sir."

"At least you get to see a piece of him every time you look at the twins."

"Yeah, I also get his attitude when I wake them up in the morning."

Both shared a laugh before Christopher asked, "You said you were seeking employment?"

"Yes, sir, I was hoping they would've called me by now."

"What is it that you did before your husband's passing?"

"I was basically a housewife tending to the kids and my plants."

Catching Christopher's ear, he inquired, "What kind of plants?"

"I had potted orchids, petunias, and a few habanero plants hanging from the balcony. Living at the condo, I didn't have a backyard or else I would have had a nice sized garden."

"Would you be interested in the manager position overseeing the five massive greenhouses, and also allowing me to accommodate you with a two bedroom in which I will have bunkbeds installed for the boys?"

Beside herself with tears of happiness flowing, "Oh, God, yes," she exclaimed.

"Now, the rent will be $33 and the water is $7 for the total sum of $40 a month. The entire complex is solar powered and you have free cable. Our strict policy is zero tolerance for drugs and alcohol on the premises. Last but not least, I also require that you pray daily."

"Not a problem," Yuki replied, revealing her shiny silver rosary she had tucked away in her pocket.

"That's beautiful," Chris said with a smile. "The meals are free for the first month. After that you will be required to pay a dollar for your meal because the children will eat free for the duration of your stay. The managerial position pays a base salary of $1,500 a month. Once you get settled in you can begin working."

Still in awe from the blessing, she smiled through streams of tears. "May God continue to bless you, Christopher."

Deacon Bob was leading the charge with 10 rented U-Haul trucks at the ready and a throng of volunteers to help these women get moved in.

Sending Yuki on her way and into the helping hands of many volunteers, Christopher then turned his gaze upon the next woman in line.

The day would go on with more of the same happening. Christopher would hear the stories of these heartbroken, strong-willed women going through hardships in need of a much overdue blessing.

One by one, Christopher would slide them the one-year contract charging a total sum of $40 a month with cable included. He would take them at their word that they would not use drugs or alcohol and pray daily.

The complex was filling up fast with almost half of the 210 apartments already occupied. Becoming overwhelmed and not wanting to turn a mother in need away just to come back tomorrow, help finally arrived in the form of an older, short in stature, elegant Latina, a streak of silver in her flowing black hair that reminded him of Ma'.

Speaking in her sweet tone, "Hello, I'm Suzanne. I'm a retired widow with no children. The rent was raised at my residence a hundred dollars six months ago. Just last Friday I received a letter informing me my rent would increase another hundred dollars starting next month. I'm struggling to barely pay it now with my pension."

"The world can be cruel sometimes. Trust me, I can relate. What was your occupation before retiring?"

"I worked in the fraud department at the local bank."

"So, you're a people person and a good judge of character."

"I like to think so," replied Suzanne.

"Your voice is really sweet, and I can tell you have a good heart."

"Thank you for the kind words. It's funny you mention my voice. My mother actually nicknamed me Cookie on account of how sweet she said I sounded."

"Do you mind if I call you Cookie from now on?"

"No, not at all."

Smiling, Christopher continued. "Cookie, I would like to make you copilot in bringing these women home. I'm offering you a job at the front desk to help place occupants in these vacancies."

Handing her keys to a two bedroom on the first floor, "The salary is $1,200 a month and you will only be helping me, as I will take the bulk of the work. The total sum is $40 a month for rent with the promise of daily prayer, should you accept my offer."

"I'm a Christian, so the prayer box is checked. Now are you sure the cost for rent is $40 a month?"

"Yes, ma'am, 1000 percent sure."

"And you are going to pay me $1,200 a month to help you at the front desk?"

"Yes, ma'am. So is that a yes?"

"Of course, it's a yes, and I can start now," Cookie replied.

"Well welcome to day one of your new

life. Go ahead and come around the desk and have a seat so you can learn the process while getting a feel for how to accommodate the ladies."

Taking her seat, all Cookie could do was smile knowing the blessing she'd received placed her in a position to bless others time and time again.

CHAPTER THIRTEEN

Christopher's life was pretty much on full display due to the bombing and the loss of his family to the senseless, evil act. He himself had become a godsend to many, especially the single mothers, widows, and homeless.

It was on the fourth day of the opening week that Christopher came face-to-face with a woman dressed in an all-black hijab covered head to toe. Only her black skin and dark brown eyes were revealed through a tiny slit in her face covering. Wielding two adolescent boys, each wearing a black kufi, introducing herself as Sanya, she told of her plight for the last two years struggling as a widow.

Staring intently into Christopher's eyes she spoke solemnly, "I know what happened to your wife and child and I'm truly sorry for your loss. Just know that I would not be here if I didn't need help."

Without hesitation Christopher replied, "I'm sorry to inform you, but I cannot properly accommodate you at this time."

"Is it because I am a Muslim, and you consider this payback for what has happened to your family?"

"No, ma'am, it's because I only have a two-bedroom vacancy, and I can clearly see that you are in much need of a three bedroom. These growing boys certainly need their space."

"Why do you say this?"

"I can put you into a two bedroom in the meantime, and as soon as a three bedroom becomes available you will be the next tenant to retain it."

"Are you serious? We can stay here?"

"Yes, ma'am, the rent is $40 a month and that includes cable for the boys."

Taking a deep breath, he continued, "Please understand I hold no ill will towards your religion or beliefs. I only wish I had a vacant three bedroom for you today."

"You have no idea how much the two bedrooms will be accommodating. My boys and I thank you from the bottom of our hearts."

"As a Muslim, I'm aware that you're required to pray five times a day, so there should be no problem with my request that you pray daily. I just believe that the more a person prays it will increase that personal relationship with God, making them a better person."

"I agree with your philosophy."

Smiling, Christopher continued, "After all, it was Mother Teresa who said every Christian is called to be a good Christian. A Muslim, a good Muslim, a Hindu, a good Hindu, and so on and so forth."

"A wise woman she was," Sanya replied.

"There are plenty of volunteers to help

you get moved in. Just let them know your apartment number."

Sanya signaled to her sons to come over as she thanked Christopher again for his kindness.

"You know, I heard that the Virgin Mary has her own book in the Quran."

"Yes, she has her own sura."

"Maybe one day you can show me?"

"Whenever you'd like, just let me know," Sanya replied with a smile from ear to ear underneath her hijab.

CHAPTER FOURTEEN

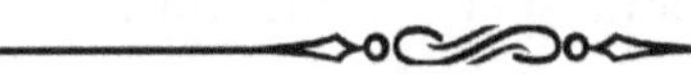

That first weekend had been quite a sight to behold. Stepping off to the side, Christopher watched as the tenants served the homeless in Angelica's Taste of Heaven restaurant, bringing tears to his eyes as he witnessed a utopia of sorts with charity at the core of their hearts and principle thought.

Receiving jobs along with apartments had allowed these women to find their footing in the world and begin to make their mark starting with serving the less fortunate.

After the homeless had been fed and the restaurant cleaned, it was then that the women and children sat down to eat. Without a spoken word or direction, God had brought his people together and placed them in their proper position.

❖   ❖   ❖

With the start of a new week Christopher only had a few more vacancies left to fill before he could spend more time in the greenhouses cultivating his passion.

Approaching the front desk was a young, petite, light-skinned Latina with dyed purple hair cropped around her cute face. Reeking of marijuana smoke, Chris thought that explained her bloodshot eyes, glancing at the colored ink that saturated her neck and left hand all the way up to her elbow as she put her toddler son down. Bypassing the pleasantries, she asked through a pierced lip, "How much is a one bedroom?"

"This complex doesn't have one

bedrooms, only twos and threes."

Frustrated, she replied with an attitude, "So then how much is it for a two?"

"First off, what's your name?"

"Jessica, and I work at the daycare next to the Kroger."

"Okay, Jessica, I'm Christopher and you should know we have rules at this complex."

"And what are the rules?"

"We have a zero-tolerance policy for possessing illegal drugs or alcohol on the premises."

"Hold on, mister. If I'm paying rent what makes you think you can dictate how I choose to live my life? This is America and I make my own choices. Last time I checked alcohol was legal for anyone over 21 and I'm 23."

Christopher made a sharp reply, "That is certainly true. You can choose to be rich or poor, smart or dumb, and a homeowner or homeless. So, what is it going to be? Obviously, your decisions so far have you standing before me frustrated with the weight of the world sitting on your shoulders."

"And who are you to judge?" With a smirk on her face Jessica began to vent, "My son's deadbeat dad has paid child support four times. Well, that's how many months he worked before he got locked up. I work a minimum wage job with screaming kids all day. So yeah, I relieve the stress with a little smoke and drink. You make it seem like I'm a bad person or something."

"You're a strong woman and all the strong Latinas in my life have raised strong men, so why would I see you any different? I only want to offer you an opportunity to create your own path in life, and as long as you're drunk and high you will remain lost. I'm offering you an apartment and a managerial position running our daycare. Rent will be $40 a month and your salary will be $1,500 a month, should you accept."

Looking intently into her eyes, Chris continued, "Now you have choices you have to make for you and your son. Are you going to be sober and smart, allowing yourself to accumulate some savings, affording you the opportunity to buy a home in the near future? Or do you want to be high and dumb as you continue to suffer through the struggle of living check to check, raising a toddler on a downward spiral with no end in sight?"

A smile invaded Jessica's face as she asked, "You really see a strong woman in me?"

"Of course, I do. You just need to open your eyes so that you can see it. Signing this year-long contract will guarantee everything we discussed. Also, there is a requirement that you pray daily. For this I will take you at your word, and if you haven't prayed before today, then know there's a first for everything."

Jessica sarcastically replied, "And there it is. I knew there was a catch. I don't believe in God, or your God, to be exact. I'm an atheist, and if you've been through what I've gone through then you would be too."

"I've been to hell and back a few times. That's exactly why I believe in God," Christopher spoke sternly. "In all seriousness, I didn't say you must pray to my God. I said you are required to pray. I don't care if you believe the bees and the flowers pollinated you into being or that the constellations collided in the colossal big bang theory. Whatever wakes you up in the morning thanking that entity for a new day, just continue to do just that. If it's the butterfly or cow that you choose to worship, then so be it."

Seeing her face soften again, Christopher continued, "You see, prayer is communication with your creator, and if you truly believe in an intergalactic life-giving event, then stand on that. As for me and my household, we shall worship the Lord. I believe the one true God will reveal Himself to all in His perfect timing. So, I ask that you pray even if it is to the clock on the wall."

"Mister, I didn't expect all this when I walked through that door this morning."

"This is just the tip of the iceberg. Follow me, I have something I want to show you. You can leave your son with Cookie. Trust me, he will be in good hands."

Passing her son along to a smiling lady, Jessica then followed Christopher to a thick metal door with a black plaque that read

"CRASH ROOM" in white letters.

Using his key on the deadbolt, Christopher then closed and locked the door after they'd entered. Looking around the large room, Jessica was shocked to see smashed up appliances, chairs, bicycles, computer monitors, and televisions.

"What's all this junk for?"

Christopher proceeded to hand her a clear face shield and a pair of gloves. "Here, put these on." Strapping his hands in his gloves he then grabbed two stainless steel bats, passing her one, and said, "Now watch and learn."

Adjusting his shield, he began swinging the bat at the black bicycle frame that lay at his feet, knocking several dents into the metal frame with his powerful swings. Turning to his right he smashed the front of a computer monitor sitting on the floor, sending glass flying eight different directions.

Spent, Christopher spoke through breaths, "Now it's your turn."

Taking a page from his book, Jessica wound back her bat and swung with all her might, obliterating the small 20-inch flat screen with a single homerun hit, sending most of the pieces into the far wall.

"Keep on," Chris energetically exclaimed. "The room is soundproof, so scream as you swing," letting out a deep roar himself to demonstrate, "Ayyyye."

Screaming at the top of her lungs, Jessica shattered a blender into a thousand pieces before swinging mercilessly at a microwave in between gut-wrenching screams.

Exerting all her energy into smashing everything in sight for the last three minutes with the metal bat had caused Jessica to release her anger and bitter mood, finding herself on her knees, shaking as she clenched the bat. Her face shield was fogged from heavy breathing and uncontrollable tears.

Seeing her broken on the floor, Christopher knew it was now time to build her back up. He started with words of encouragement, "Let it out, whatever it is, get it out of your system. Cleanse your soul, Jessica. Tomorrow you'll wake up sober, renewed, and ready to conquer the world."

Picking her up off the ground,

Christopher gave her a hug. "Life is what we make of it. So, I need the best of you. Your son needs the best of you. Humanity needs the best of you. All the drugs and alcohol ever do is take the best of you."

Removing her face shield, Christopher looked into her watery eyes. "Who would you rather share the best of you with? Your son or the drugs and alcohol?"

"My son," she replied in her whispery, teary tone.

"Now let's get you back on track so you can take control of your path in life." Seeing a rejuvenated spirit come to life within her, Chris continued, "Jessica, I need to know, are you going to be my new tenant and daycare manager?"

Through tears of joy she exclaimed, "Yes, sir, thank you, Christopher," while giving him a hug.

"That's a good answer. Now when you go to work today you can give them your two weeks' notice."

Jessica smiled as Christopher handed her a Kleenex from the box he kept next to the broken and beaten black couch with the cut-up cushions.

"I had this crash room secretly inserted into the blueprints so I could crash out when I needed. Remind me to get you a key made so you can have unlimited access."

"I'd like that," replied Jessica.

"Let's return to the front desk. I know your son is missing you, and Cookie will give you the key to your new apartment."

✦

Chapter Fifteen

It was a Friday afternoon when the tenants came together to prepare various ethnic foods combining cultural and religion-based traditions to make for a lavish and festive feast as a way to say thank you to the volunteers for all their help, but most of all to Christopher.

With their bellies full the volunteers dispersed to the five greenhouses containing 10,000 plants in each. The plants yielding an average of 2.3 pounds would meet the quarterly demand of 100,000 pounds of Chriang peppers. Requiring all hands on deck, the hundreds of tenants and volunteers harvested and packaged the Chriang peppers to be shipped to the Wings That Sting corporation as per the contractual agreement, generating the revenue to operate High Hopes and pay salaries.

Yuki had the assembly line running like a well-oiled machine. The hundred pound boxes of jalapenos were stacked on pallets and taped down while a forklift would load the pallets onto a flat bed trailer, ready for delivery.

Pulling Frank to the side, Chris said, "Who would of ever guessed that we would be witnessing a dream come true?"

"You got a point, my brother. I'm just grateful you brought me along for the ride. Speaking of a ride," reaching into his pocket to retrieve a key with a Mercedes emblem, then handing it to Christopher, "this is for you."

"That new Mercedes you drove up in. You're giving it to me?" asked Chris.

"Yes, sir, consider it a token of appreciation. Deacon Bob will drive me home."

"Thank you, bro. Well, it seems we're exactly where we're supposed to be in life."

"I couldn't agree with you more, my brother."

"While we are on the subject of life, Frank, when are you going to settle down and begin the next chapter of your life?"

"Funny you should ask," smiled Frank, "I've actually met someone. She moved down here from North Carolina a few months ago and just recently began attending our church. She's a beautiful Latina, intelligent, and funny. We've only been dating three weeks, but I think I'm in love."

"Why isn't she here with us so I could meet her?"

"She's attending school to become a nurse, taking day and night classes to speed up the process. The ladies prepared a plate for me to take to her."

"So, I guess the real question is, why haven't you purchased a ring yet?"

"I just want to make sure she's the right

one."

"Oh, trust me, she's definitely the right one for you. I've never seen that gleam in your eye when you spoke about any other girl you dated. So, quit wasting time and make it official and enjoy life together."

"You make a valid point. First thing in the morning I'll find her the perfect diamond ring and propose on Sunday after Mass."

"Angelica and I were married just three months after meeting. I only wish I'd married my angel sooner. Just know God brought this beautiful woman into your life for a reason."

"I will spend all morning finding the perfect symbol of love."

"After Mass on Sunday I'll have a small get-together at my house where you can pop the question. There will be plenty of food and friends to share in your blissful joy."

"Sounds good to me, my brother."

Christopher was happy that he could play a role in Frank's proposal. He then inquired, "By the way, Frank, what's this beautiful woman's name?"

Caught up in the moment of it all, he

replied with a smile, "Irene, her name is Irene."

"Well, when you take her the plate of food you tell my future sister-in-law I look forward to meeting her at Mass on Sunday morning."

CHAPTER SIXTEEN

As the wind blows touching all of earth's surfaces, an endless stream of time foreshadows the events, leaving behind its imprint through erosion and pollination, breathing life to God's creation with graceful beauty and mystique.

So, it too was with each passing generation. Serving out his calling to works of charity for over two decades had Christopher looking to fulfill his final promise to Neveah by purchasing a black and brown Yorkie puppy from the pet store.

The cashier handed back Christopher's debit card as he said, "Enjoy your new puppy, sir."

"Thank you, and I will," Christopher replied, walking out of the pet store with a bag of dog food and his new best friend.

Two years prior Deacon Bob was called home, and Christopher was still reeling from the heartache of the untimely passing of Padre Perez. Christopher had been through a lot, and for the first time since burying his beloved father figure six months ago he'd finally cracked a smile as he glanced over at the puppy.

Meeting Padre Perez's successor, Padre Evaristeo, a young Mexican American with a medium build and a military style haircut. He was Christopher's height and had presided at Padre Perez's funeral. They quickly became friends as the young priest had a great fervor for the Lord and his flock.

Over the last two decades Christopher, now 73 years of age, had helped several single mothers and countless widows, many of whom went on to purchase their own homes, extending a helping hand to friends, family, and even strangers in need. The gift that kept on giving time and time again would leave an indention in the world and continue to reverberate throughout the earth in the form of ripples of love to God's children. Having to endure the pain of burying his friends and brothers and sisters in Christ was all part of the routine for the past two decades.

Nevertheless, Christopher never broke stride with his calling in anticipation of reuniting with his loved ones for eternity.

Glancing over at the cute puppy sitting in the passenger seat, Christopher voiced, "I'm going to name you Cash because who doesn't love money? And once people lay their eyes on you they will instantly fall in love."

Cash looked up at Christopher with his big brown eyes and began to wag his pudgy tail.

"Okay, Cash, time to take you home," Chris said as he started the car.

CHAPTER SEVENTEEN

Christopher was a vibrant old man with a weathered heart, clean shaven and a head full of short, white hair. He sat at the front desk with his eyes closed, reclining in the comfortable chair. It was reasonably quiet but for the short bursts of barks coming from Cash periodically.

Startled by the commotion of a young girl's giggle and innocent voice, "Mister, what's your puppy's name?"

Christopher sat up to see an adorable

young girl with big round, brown eyes resembling copper pennies cradling Cash in her arms.

"Mary, come here this instant. What have I told you about running off?" scorned her mother.

"But mommy, look at the puppy."

"And put the puppy down right now."

"Yes, ma'am," replied the little girl, doing as she was told.

"Sir, I apologize, she lives in her own little world."

"It's fine," Chris said with a smile as he rose to his feet to shake the hand of the young Latino standing before him.

"Hello, sir, I'm Manuel Molina and this is my wife Benina and daughter Mary."

"Nice to meet you, I'm Christopher. What can I do for you today?"

"Well, sir, my wife and I are Catholics and second-generation Mexican Americans. We moved to Austin from Houston a few weeks ago so Benina could attend the University of Texas and graduate with a degree in business management. I myself am a hard worker, which brings me to the reason I'm here."

Cash gave out a soft bark as Mary patted him on the head.

"His name is Cash," Chris said as Mary beamed with joy.

Manuel continued, "You see, sir, we've heard of your generosity back home and I was hoping that you could offer me a job and possibly an apartment so we could get out of the motel."

"What is it that you know how to do?"

"For the last five years I've worked as an electrician with my father. I also know how to install flooring and minor plumbing. I believe I can be a good handyman to you as I know my way around tools."

"You said that y'all are currently staying at a motel?"

"Yes, sir, the Motel 6."

"Well, that's no place for a family to live. I could use a handyman because we've been operating for over 20 years and there's a lot of wear and tear on these apartments. Unfortunately, I don't have any vacancies."

Having a good feeling about this young family, Christopher continued, "What I do propose is that y'all stay at my house as my guests until I can get y'all properly housed."

"Oh, no, sir, we couldn't impose on your life like that," Manuel abruptly replied.

"The way I see it, this affords us the opportunity to get to know each other, especially if we are going to be working together. That is, if you want the job. Plus, I have plenty of room and Mary can keep Cash company because I surely can't keep up with him."

Benina batted her eyes at her husband as Manuel casually shook his head in a yes motion. Shaking Christopher's hand as he spoke, "We'll gladly take you up on your offer, sir, and thank you for your generosity."

"No problem, now let's get your belongings from that motel and get y'all settled in." Passing Manuel his cell phone, "Enter your number and I'll text you the address."

CHAPTER EIGHTEEN

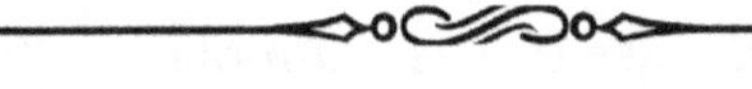

Pulling into the circular driveway of the luxurious multimillion dollar estate, all of Christopher's house guests were breathless from taking in the sheer size and beauty of the home.

The first one to exit the vehicle was Mary who ran straight to Cash, scooping him up in her arms. Christopher was standing at the front door watching Mary giggle as Cash jumped around in her arms while licking her face.

Looking up at Christopher, Mary asked, "Do you have a pool?"

"Yes, I do," replied Chris, "Can you swim?"

"No, I haven't learned yet, but I want to."

"We can certainly fix that problem"

Mary smiled from ear to ear and Cash began to bark, wagging his pudgy, furry tail as if in agreement.

"Sir, is this really your home that you're allowing us to stay in?" inquired Benina.

"Yes, ma'am, and please call me Chris. Benina, one of my family's favorite nuns had the same name."

"Wow, I'll take that as a compliment, and Chris, I've never seen a home so grand."

Manuel walked up to Chris with his hand extended. "Thank you again for your generosity. I promise I will work hard and not let you down."

Shaking hands, Chris replied, "I always trust my spiritual intuition, and I believe you're a man of your word that wants the best for your family. So, consider this day one of a new beginning."

Entering the mansion, Christopher

pointed to the golden, curving, cascading staircase. "There are seven vacant rooms, so please choose which ever best suits your taste."

Wasting no time, Benina and Mary with Cash in tow scaled the cascading stairs, excitement fueling them as they converged on every room, allowing the intricate splendor of ornate décor to steal their wide-eyed attention.

It took quite some time before they made their choices and Manuel had their luggage accounted for.

Chris had taken the liberty of ordering pizza so that they could enjoy the rest of the day.

With their bellies full, Christopher set up Mary and Cash in the theater to watch the new "Lion King" movie. He wanted an uninterrupted conversation with Manuel and Benina.

Sitting in the living room sipping sweet tea they relaxed, allowing their food to settle. Christopher began to state, "I know at this moment you're grateful for the help and may think that you were the ones in most need when you walked in that door today. That is only half true because two weeks ago our long-time maintenance man Joe and his wife Liz left for greener pastures along with their four kids. They had family that needed them to help out back home in San Antonio. I for one believe family is everything, so as I was sad to see them go, I know it was for the greater good."

Smiling at the young couple, Christopher continued. "Now God has answered my prayers yet again. As you can see, I'm an old man who is limited in the maintenance department."

"I'm here to do whatever needs to be done," Manuel said with a straight face.

Shifting focus to Benina, Christopher inquired, "And what about you? Do you enjoy cooking?"

"Oh, yes, sir. I learned from my mother and she's a great cook. I'll be graduating next year and I'm hoping to land a head position managing the day-to-day operations at a big corporation. Manuel and I have the same vision of what we want for our family, so we are committed to putting in the hard work needed to see our vision of success come to fruition."

"Would you be opposed to helping out at High Hopes in the kitchen on the weekends when we feed the homeless and also with the front desk dealing with the tenants?"

"Of course not, Chris, I would be delighted, and it would actually help me brush up on my people skills. Also, God knows I was raised by a devout Catholic mother, so charity runs through my veins."

Smiling, Christopher continued, "I will compensate you for your work at High Hopes at a salary of $1,200 a month. Y'all will stay here rent free until something becomes available."

Manuel interjected, "Please Christopher, you're too kind. We must pay you rent as long as we reside here."

"Trust me, you will work it off in due time. I have a quaint three bedroom house that I own. It needs some work done to it before you and your family can move in. We will drive over to see it tomorrow during lunch break and reconvene to settle on the terms of the agreement."

"Sounds good to me, Chris, and I look forward to getting to work tomorrow."

Glancing at his watch then back to his newfound friends he politely said, "It's getting late and I must pray the rosary before I go to bed, so…"

"Would you mind, Chris, if we joined you in praying the rosary?" Benina chimed in?

"No, not at all," replied Christopher.

"Good, let me get Mary, be back in a minute."

With everyone grasping their rosary and their eyes closed taking in the solemnity of the moment, Christopher heard Mary's innocent voice recite the rosary prayers, sending his heart racing into overdrive as the beats palpitated, drumming tears out of his soulful eyes and down the weather-beaten, soft crevices of his cheeks.

It was like he could hear Nevaeh's voice praying for him in heaven. An angel's voice had finally filled the house.

In that instant Christopher knew everything was as it was meant to be, including this divine happenstance.

CHAPTER NINETEEN

It was lunch time and Manuel and Christopher were on their way to view the house.

Manuel had been on his feet all morning fixing problems in a dozen apartments, leaving an impactful impression on Chris leading him to believe strongly in the pull on his heart to help out this young family as much as possible.

During their commute Chris would learn that Mary was six years old, and her birthday was the same day as the Immaculate Conception. December 8 is the celebration of the sinless birth of the blessed Virgin Mary in preparation of becoming the pure vessel for the untainted, sinless birth of Jesus Christ.

With Mary's seventh birthday only a month away, Chris wasted no time in talking Manuel into agreeing to allow him to give her a birthday party at the house fit for a princess.

Pulling into the driveway, Manuel felt so blessed to have these opportunities come about for his family. Seeing the house for the first time he instantly fell in love. Walking inside he felt right at home, and he was happy to see the house was spacious enough to hold his young family. After a quick surveyance, it was time to finalize the requirements.

Turning his gaze to Christopher Manual said, "I can't wait to show Benina this house. Now, what exactly are your terms?"

"I own this house and I would gladly sign it over to you if you agree to work for five years as maintenance man at the complex.

I would see that as sufficient payment for this home, which is valued at $190,000. Y'all will stay with me rent free, and with the salary Benina earns for helping out at High Hopes you should have enough to carry y'all through the years."

Excitedly Manuel replied, "I agree to the terms, and Chris, I can't thank you enough for this gift."

Shaking hands, Chris stated, "As I said, it has minor work to be done but all that can be assessed over time. Quite frankly, I enjoy the company, so I would hope that y'all stay for the duration of the agreement."

"We enjoy your company and conversations also, and Mary would play all day with Cash if we let her. Cash may be the only one that needs a break."

Enjoying a laugh together, Christopher placed his hand on Manuel's shoulder. "I will give my lawyer a call and have him draw up the paperwork to require your signature later this week. I'm glad we could make a deal."

"Me too, Chris. Benina is going to go crazy when I tell her the good news."

"Don't forget to tell her about the upcoming birthday party for Mary."

"Yes, sir."

"Now let's head on back and see what the ladies cooked up for lunch," Chris said as they exited Ma's house.

CHAPTER TWENTY

It was the end of the week and as promised Manuel, Benina, and Mary were meeting Frank for the first time sitting in his conference room at the huge oak table.

Laying a stack of forms before them, Manuel thought twice and said, "I thought I would be looking at a few forms and signing once, not a manuscript."

"I assure you Mr. Molina that everything here is in accordance with all that was discussed between you and Christopher. I've been in practice for over three decades, and my firm is one of the best in the country."

"No, sir, I would never question your practice or expertise. I only thought there would be less paperwork. I guess that's why I never made it to law school."

Everyone began to laugh as Frank handed Manuel and Benina a black ballpoint pen, then Frank began to turn page after page and pointing to the dotted lines that required their signatures.

Next he took the binding contract and placed it in front of Christopher, who removed his own black felt pen from the breast pocket of his black tailor-made suit.

Signing the documents, Christopher said nonchalantly, "I'm glad that's out of the way." Seeing that Mary was bored he continued, "and later on we will resume day three of Mary's swimming lessons."

"Yeah," Mary exclaimed as her face lit up.

"Today the floaties will come off and you will be swimming all on your own."

Thinking it through for a moment before

replying in her innocent voice, "Okay, I'm ready."

Christopher shook Frank's hand, "Thank you Frank for taking care of this for me on such short notice."

"Anything for you, my brother."

"Would you and Irene join us for dinner? That way they can meet Irene?"

"We'll be there."

Glancing at his watch Christopher stated, "We better be heading back to High Hopes before they notice we're gone."

"Yeah, and Cashie is probably barking wondering where I'm at."

Through everyone's laughter Chris replied, "Yeah, Mary, I'm pretty sure he is."

✦

CHAPTER TWENTY-ONE

It was as if the house had finally become a home. Christopher's heart was overflowing with love once again. They had cried and laughed together, bringing them even closer. Blissful from having played a significant part in teaching Mary how to swim and with her seventh birthday tomorrow, he looked forward to the enjoyment of making that memory.

The last month was more than Christopher could have hoped for. It was full of love for one another. Heartfelt stories were told, dreams were spoken, and hard work and dedication for their vision of success had shown daily. Overall, they had persevered as a family because that's what families do, and from day one the Molinas and Christopher had become a family.

Relishing in the fact that God brings His people together, Christopher never doubted what was to be. He instead allowed the Holy Spirit to flourish and bring everything to fruition.

Adjusting his new eyeglasses from time to time as he supervised Manuel with his medium build, short, black hair slicked back and his strong hands at work, bending over backwards with a smile on his face as he kept the tenants happy and headache-free.

Christopher delighted in seeing Benina's intellect and beauty on display as she ran the front desk. Her long, brunette hair touching the center of her back, complimenting her graceful approach to dealing with the current tenants. She oversaw the restaurant and the packaging and distribution of the Chriang peppers in all of the five greenhouses.

Having been homeschooled by her mother until she reached middle school enabled Benina to flow seamlessly, teaching the curriculum in the classroom to the young students including Mary. With a handful of teachers the students were more engaged. Benina excelled in every department all while achieving her degree.

❖   ❖   ❖

Having been given a new beat to the tempo of his old ticker Christopher found himself in his room looking to vanquish his hold on the past.

Startled by Mary's voice and a bark from Cash, he turned to see Mary pointing at the jewelry box on the dresser as she asked, "What's in the box?"

"My two most valuable possessions," Christopher replied.

"Can I see?" Mary asked, standing on her tippy toes hoping to be tall enough to peak inside as Christopher opened the box.

Retrieving both the rings, Christopher

first showed her his wife's diamond ring. Seeing her big brown eyes light up he then showed her Nevaeh's ring.

"Wow," Mary exclaimed, "you have a Wonder Woman ring."

"It belonged to my daughter. She was your age when she passed away."

"God really loved and missed her a lot."

"Why do you say that?" Chris inquired.

"Because He wanted her back so soon," she replied in her innocent tone.

Before Chris could speak Benina's voice carried throughout the house calling for Mary.

"Come on, Cashie, mommy wants us," waving bye to Chris as she exited the room with tiny paws pitter-pattering behind her.

Without giving it a second thought, Christopher retrieved the small, blue cloth bag, untying the drawstring to spring it open.

Pouring out the tooth into his palm as he entered the restroom, tossing the small bag into the toilet, he took a moment to examine the tooth as he concluded that he no longer wished to harbor anything having to do with evil, including any intent on his part. Having found a family again he wanted to part ways with anything that wasn't coming from a place of love.

Dropping the tooth into the toilet he watched as it sank to the bottom. Taking a deep breath, he let go of the grudge he'd carried all of those years while at the same time allowing his soul to come back to life.

Flushing the toilet, he then made his way to bed knowing that his loved ones in heaven were smiling. He laid down, finally free from resentment.

CHAPTER TWENTY-TWO

Seven years young today was all that was on Mary's mind. Anticipating her birthday party, she was full of glee.

After everyone ate breakfast and Benina finished cleaning the kitchen, they all retreated to the living room to pray the rosary.

A resounding "amen" was said before Benina glanced over at the birthday girl. "Take Cash upstairs to your room. I will be coming up in a minute because both of you need a bath."

"Yes, momma," Mary replied as she

scooped up Cash in her arms before heading up the stairs.

Chris turned on the TV to CNN only to hear the news anchor announce, "Breaking news, Abdul-Akbar Hasan, the homegrown terrorist who placed the bomb that blew up the St. Peter's Catholic Church more than 20 years ago killing three church-goers, was found dead this morning in his cell.

After decades in a maximum-security prison, he died from a severe heart attack late last night, prison officials said in a statement released this morning. The FBI concluded Abdul-Akbar's motive for the bombing was him fiercely wanting to attack the first ever Christian institution and its believers."

Clicking off the TV Christopher set the remote down on the glass coffee table.

"He finally died," Benina said in her Spanish accent.

Chris thought to himself he was so glad he purged that evil stronghold from his life last night.

"We all have to answer for what we do in this life," stated Manuel. "So, it's best to do what's right all the time."

"These are true and wise words," implied

Chris.

Wanting to clear out the gloom in the room Benina smiled at Christopher, "Well, to bring back the good vibes in light of the party this afternoon, we have good news we would like to share with you, Chris. This also happens to be part of Mary's birthday present."

Standing next to his wife with his left arm around her shoulder, Manuel then took his right hand and placed it on her protruding tummy.

"We're pregnant with twins," she exclaimed.

"Twins!" Christopher joyfully replied.

"Yes, twins, can you believe it?" Benina said in her Spanish accent.

"Wow, that's a beautiful blessing. I'm so happy for y'all."

Benina continued, "We are 12 weeks pregnant and we're having a boy and a girl. As a way to say thank you for all the love and generosity you have shown us," pausing to take a deep breath, seeing as how she was breathing for three, "You're a huge part of this family, and to pay you homage my husband and I have come to an understanding that in order to truly be alive and obtain keys to the Heavenly Kingdom you must align yourself accordingly with God's word. Christopher, you've taught us that you're not truly alive until you realize that…Living Is Spiritual Awakening!"

Benina smiled and gave Chris a moment to register everything she'd said before stating, "So, we are going to use that acronym to name our daughter Lisa Nevaeh and our son will be named Xzavier Caleb after Manuel's father and my favorite country singer."

Chubby tears of happiness rolled out from behind his high-end glasses and down those wrinkled cheeks leaving Christopher speechless.

"So, what do you think?" asked Benina.

"I love it, my God, how I love it. You have no idea how much this means to me."

"We just want you to know how much you mean to us. We are family," Manuel said with a smile, "and family is forever."

Taking his wife's hand Manuel continued, "Now, let's go upstairs and tell Mary and Cash the good news. Then we have to get ready for Mass to celebrate the Immaculate Conception."

CHAPTER TWENTY-THREE

Deacon Marco had taken up the post at St. Peter's after Deacon Bob's passing. A Mexican American with a muscular build stemming from a decade of body building competitions, he kept a shaved head and full black beard. Although his look was intimidating at first glance, he was an extremely humble man.

His stunning wife LeAnn was a beautiful African American woman. Her flawless mahogany skin and shoulder length, straight black hair complimented her light brown eyes and loving attitude. It was as if she was born for the role of a deacon's wife. Along with their son and daughter, they showed up early to lend a hand before everyone arrived.

The party was truly fit for a princess and everything Mary had hoped for and more. She enjoyed the miniature pony she had requested and was in awe of the huge tiara cake with white and pink frosting.

Friends from church and High Hopes were in attendance which brought the guest count to well over a hundred with about half being children.

Mary was having the time of her young life and left everyone amazed at her actions after she'd opened all her presents. Her little heart was determined to bring joy to others. Mary first pulled out two presents from the multitude of gifts she'd received, handing them to Benina, "Momma these are for Lisa and Xzavier when they get here."

Next, she proceeded to hand a gift to each of the children in attendance, most of whom voiced that they would be following Mary's lead and doing the same thing at their next birthday party.

The adults watched idly by, beside themselves, experiencing an awe moment for they knew they were in the presence of a young angel.

Feeling inspired, Padre Evaristeo turned to Deacon Marco, "That little angel just gave me a homily to use at next year's celebration of the Immaculate Conception."

Deacon Marco glanced over at his wife only to see LeAnn dabbing at the tears welling up in the corners of her loving eyes with her thumbs. Walking over he gave her a hug, whispering in her ear, "Baby, it's time to break the pinata."

❖　　　❖　　　❖

That evening Frank and Irene were the last of the guests to leave. After saying their goodbyes Chris closed the front door then summoned everyone to the living room to pray the rosary before calling it a night.

Cash sat next to Mary quiet as can be with everybody ready to begin praying, eyes closed, holding their rosary.

"Wait just a moment," Chris interjected,

"I almost forgot," pulling out a hand-sized, white box with red bow from his pants pocket, handing it to Mary who was overjoyed. "Happy seventh birthday, Mary."

Ecstatic she rushed to open the box revealing a golden rosary. Jumping up she hugged Christopher and kissed him on the cheek exclaiming, "It's just like yours, Chris. It's so beautiful, thank you very much."

"You're welcome. Now, are you ready?"

"Yes, sir," Mary replied in a joyous tone.

"Good, then let us pray."

Concluding the prayer everyone hugged and spoke of their love for one another before saying goodnight.

Retiring to his room alone because Cash would sleep with Mary, his favorite companion, Chris thought to himself, "So much for man's best friend."

Setting his golden rosary on the night stand he then climbed into bed. Pulling the covers up to his chest he clasped his hands and began to pray, "Thank you God for giving me a fruitful life and granting me the desires of my heart. Thank you for all that you do in my life and never leaving my side. I only hope I made you smile, Father." Making the sign of the cross with his right hand he said aloud, "Amen."

With his eyes closed Christopher began to smile at the thought of having made God smile at least once throughout his lifetime.

CHAPTER TWENTY-FOUR

Preparing breakfast Benina happened to glance at the clock in the kitchen. Noticing it was 10 'til 7 had her wondering why Christopher wasn't sitting at the table enjoying a black cup of coffee by now.

Manuel kissed his wife on the cheek as she stood at the stove scrambling eggs. After scanning the kitchen, he asked, "Where's Chris?"

"I don't know, baby, maybe he slept in after all the excitement from the party. He's usually up every day at 6 a.m."

"I'm going to let him know the food's almost ready and his coffee is waiting. Plus, he has to get ready for Mass. I know he doesn't want to miss out on Mass."

"Call the little one down also, baby."

"Yes, ma'am," replied Manuel as he exited the kitchen heading for the staircase, opting not to use the elevators.

Manuel called out to his daughter before knocking on Christopher's door. Receiving no answer, he proceeded to enter the room, seeing Christopher still lying in bed. He spoke in a soft tone, "Time to get up, Chris. Benina is preparing your cup of coffee as we speak."

Still receiving no reply, Manuel then walked over and gently patted Chris on the shoulder to awaken him from his deep slumber.

Realizing his body was stiff with the movement of dead weight, Manuel placed his palm over his friend's nose to see if he was breathing.

Feeling no air stream, he swallowed hard as his eyes began to water. Glancing at his dear friend's face he looked to be smiling. Manuel's heart fluttered because he knew Christopher was home with his family in eternal bliss.

Startled by Mary's innocent voice, "Daddy where are you?" as she approached the room from down the hall, Manuel rushed to the door closing it behind him. Mary stood before him holding Cash. "Daddy we are hungry," she proclaimed before asking, "Can Cash come to Mass with us today if he promises not to bark?"

"Princess, let's go downstairs, your mother is looking for you."

Looking up at her father's wet eyes she asked, "Daddy are you okay? Where's Christopher?"

Picking up his daughter Manuel kissed her on the forehead and replied, "Yes, mija, everything is okay."

Reaching the kitchen Manuel set Mary down with her still cradling Cash telling her, "Look in the pantry and see if Cash has any dog food left."

Doing as she was told Mary put Cash down and walked towards the pantry.

Manuel walked up behind Benina and whispered in her ear, "Christopher passed away in his sleep last night," placing his hands on her shoulders to comfort her and let her know everything will be alright.

In that instant Benina stopped whipping the

eggs with the spatula and was now fighting back tears, not wanting to alert Mary to something being wrong.

"I need you to take Mary out of the house while I take care of everything here, my love," Manuel whispered again.

Clenching her jaw while taking a hard swallow, Benina fought hard to hold it together. She turned off the pilot on the stove and wiped her leaking eyes dry.

"Daddy there's only a little bit left in the bag and Cashie is really hungry."

"Okay, mija, you and Cash are going to go with mommy to get some more dog food and donuts and chocolate milk for breakfast."

"Mmmm, donuts," Mary exclaimed as Cash began to bark with excitement.

Benina, still with her back to Mary, muttered out, "Let me grab my purse. You and Cash be ready to go when I get back."

"Yes, mommy," replied Mary.

After cleaning up her face and catching her breath, Benina headed back downstairs to get Mary and Cash out of the house while Manuel attended to Christopher.

CHAPTER TWENTY-FIVE

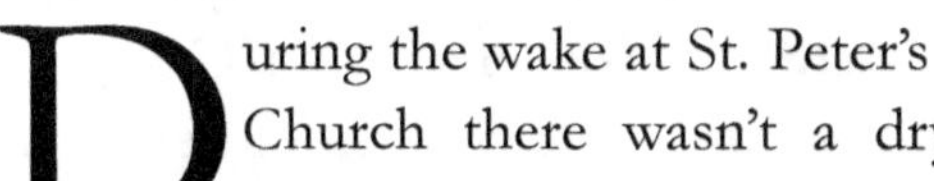

During the wake at St. Peter's Catholic Church there wasn't a dry eye in sight for what seemed to stretch on forever. For as far as the eye could see droves of people came out to pay their respects to Christopher.

There wasn't a break to be had in the countless generous acts that Christopher doled out, with so many people telling heartfelt stories of love and compassion that Christopher bestowed time and time again. One by one they told of the blessings they'd received at a time when they were at their lowest. Men and women from different races, religions, and creeds all spoke of Christopher so lovingly that many wondered how they could still produce tears after all the crying they'd already done.

Suddenly everyone's eyes began to focus on the two black gentlemen in black suits wearing black kufis with full, thick beards approaching the podium. The oldest of the two introduced himself as Damen and began his eulogy by witnessing the day their widowed mother Sanya reached out to Christopher for help. Their lives had changed drastically because she had received more than she had asked for. Later that day she explained to her sons that they'd been in the company of an angel of God.

Looking out into the crowd the oldest spoke sternly, "As you can see, my brother and I are both Muslims and this good man," glancing over at Christopher laying in his casket, "never batted an eye or gave it a second thought as he dropped everything to help us. He even gave our mother a job as a teacher in the classroom, paying her for something she would of happily done for free."

Taking a deep breath, he surveyed the multitude in attendance. "Although we may not be Christians, it was our beloved mother who rooted us in Islam and Christopher who instilled in us to live out our faith as a good Muslim. I only hope he saw in us just that."

With a smile etched across his face he continued, "I believe it was Giovanni Francesco Bernadone, otherwise known to the modern world as Saint Francis of Assisi, who said Christians should preach the Gospel always and when necessary, use words. Christopher lived, breathed, and bled this statement and because of that my brother and I know the Gospel of Jesus even though neither of us has ever read the Bible."

Humbled by everyone's loving facial expressions he spoke solemnly, "I will leave you with this. Christopher shared a special bond with our mother, so on her deathbed she asked to see him. We were blessed to see our mother joyous in her last moments. Christopher paid for the funeral and the flight to have my uncle flown in to celebrate our mother's life and pay his respects. Chris always believed that family is everything. I know that many of you refer to him as a brother and various other titles."

Standing next to his brother he said with a smile, "Malik and I consider Christopher a close family member and above all a saint."

Everyone was dabbing at the endless streams of tears with Kleenex and handkerchiefs as they looked to one another, nodding in unison to a silent agreement of the notion that Christopher truly was a saint.

After Frank and Irene shared their loving stories and kind words they returned to their seats, allowing Manuel, Benina, and Mary, cradling Cash in her arms, to come forth to the podium and share their eulogy of heartfelt words with the masses in attendance. Mary set Cash down as her father began to speak. Everyone watched in amazement as Cash left Mary's side, walking over and laying at the head of Christopher's casket with his furry face pressed to the shiny, marble floor as if to pay his respects to his beloved owner.

In that moment Benina took her daughter's hand as they walked over to the clear glass casket. Looking inside through pouring tears she saw Christopher immaculately dressed in the white tux he'd worn on his wedding day. Removing Angelica's wedding ring from her purse, she placed it inside Christopher's interlocked hands resting on his chest. "You give this to your wife when you see her,

Christopher," she said through tears.

Bending down she picked up Mary by the waist so she could look down into the casket and see Chris. Mary took out the Wonder Woman ring from her pocket and placed it in Christopher's hands along with Angelica's diamond wedding ring. In her somber, innocent voice she said, "Now you can give Nevaeh back her ring." Peering back at her mother, she began to cry as her little heart drummed a flow of tears out of her big brown eyes. Benina proceeded to hug her daughter tight as she walked over to stand next to her husband who was concluding his eulogy.

Marco, LeAnn, and their son and daughter were next at the podium followed by Bishop Leon who promptly made everyone's ears perk up during his eulogy when he stated in a heavy Spanish accent, "I had the privilege of speaking with the Pope this morning. He is aware that Christopher is being dubbed the modern saint. In short, the Vatican will assist in evaluating the process of sainthood due to the outcry of the people touched by this good and virtuous man. The Pope has also instructed me to have his golden rosary enshrined in the church along with those of his loved ones."

As Bishop Leon returned to his seat Padre Evaristeo approached the podium. It was only fitting that Padre give the final eulogy and send off his brother in Christ.

The pallbearers, all dressed in white, escorted the coffin to an awaiting white horse and carriage outside the church.

The horse and carriage proceeded to move slowly down the street through the multitude of men, women, and children that stretched for miles on the way to Christopher's final resting place.

Every news media outlet was on the scene to capture all the onlookers waving with eyes full of tears as they erupted in chanting, "Saint, saint...saint!"

❖   ❖   ❖

Christopher was given a proper Catholic burial that Padre Evaristeo presided over. He was laid to rest next to his wife and daughter, and alongside Ma', his parents, and his grandfather. Benina noticed the beautiful dozen of red roses and the dozen of yellow roses that Chris would ritually bring to the gravesite of his loved ones every Saturday morning on full display. She couldn't help but think how great the world would be if every relationship emulated that degree of love.

❖   ❖   ❖

After the burial everyone reconvened at High Hopes to enjoy a feast and console each other's hearts. Entering Angelica's Taste of Heaven, they allowed the delicious aroma of Christopher's favorite brisket enchiladas to entice their noses.

It was during the feast that Frank leaned towards Manuel and said, "Would you and your family join us for lunch tomorrow? I have something I would like to share with y'all."

Nodding his head in a yes motion, "We'll be there, Frank."

"Good, Irene will prepare plenty of food, so come hungry," he smiled.

CHAPTER TWENTY-SIX

anuel pulled into the circular driveway of Frank and Irene's exquisite mansion. Unsure of their future since Christopher's passing, he gave his beautiful wife a half-hearted smile while caressing the back of her hand with his thumb.

Reading his face Benina inquired, "Do you think the contract is no longer good because Christopher's no longer here to see you fulfill your five-year obligation to work off the debt?"

"I honestly don't know, baby, I hope not. I had my heart set on receiving that house for our growing family."

"Daddy, what about Cashie?" Mary chimed in. "Can I keep Cashie?"

"Mija, I will figure everything out soon enough. We'll walk inside and hear what Frank has to say and enjoy Irene's home cooking. Now, bring Cash and no questions. Let's just listen to what he has to say."

"Yes, daddy."

Benina looked at her husband with loving eyes and smiled, "I know you will take care of us no matter what, mi amor."

Entering the mansion, they were warmly greeted by Frank and Irene then taken into the living room where a thick contract lay on the intricately carved, oak coffee table.

Seeing Manuel's face when he laid eyes on the contract Frank decided not to let the anticipation build.

"So, as you know I invited you here today to convey some information. I have been Christopher's long-time brother in Christ and his lawyer handling all business and estate affairs. So, let me get down to business because I know y'all are currently staying in the mansion."

"Yes, sir, we are, but I was hoping that the

deal Christopher and I made with the other house would still stand and we could move in there," Manuel interjected.

"Well, I don't think that would be in your best interest," Frank stated. "You see, those forms Benina and yourself signed before were and still are binding contracts Christopher had me draw up. There were many signatures required because Christopher owned a lucrative business in the Chriang LLC and the rights to the Chriang jalapeno. Also, his sprawling, multi-million-dollar estate and a portfolio of stocks and bonds in various companies."

Walking over and standing before Manuel and Benina so they could hear every word he was about to say clearly. "Manuel and Benina, you two are the sole owners to the exclusive rights of the Chriang jalapeno along with the Chriang Limited Liability Company. Also, the High Hopes apartment complex including everything on the property, Angelica's Taste of Heaven, and the greenhouses."

Standing speechless, mouths agape, and their faces expelling a look of surprise. In a state of shock all Manuel and Benina could do was listen intently as Frank continued, "Now, the mansion y'all currently reside in happens to be in Mary's name. So, I don't see any reason for y'all to move out unless Mary should choose otherwise."

Irene began to chuckle as Frank let the news settle in for a moment.

"Manuel, Benina, and Mary Molina, you three are now the heirs to all of which the late Christopher Espinosa Jr. owned or retained." Seeing the tears well up in their eyes, Frank was pleased to have played the role of passing on the good news. "Now that I have successfully executed Christopher's last will and testament there's only one thing that must be agreed upon before power can be transferred."

Looking intently into the young couple's drenched eyes he spoke solemnly. "You must agree to always run the business and High Hopes for the purpose of charity and never change the arrangements that are currently in place."

Feeling as though they were having an out-of-body experience from the nirvana of the situation, jubilant, they replied in unison, "I agree."

Cash began to bark and Mary asked, "What about Cashie, daddy? Can I keep him?"

Benina had her hands cupped over her

mouth, still in awe, while Manuel's mind was still racing to process the news.

Frank abruptly replied, "Of course Cash is all yours so long as you promise to care for him and take him swimming at least once a week."

Mary said excitedly, "Yes, sir, I promise I will."

Looking at the young couple Frank stated, "Honestly, I'm a little surprised to see that y'all are truly hearing this news for the first time. I was sure that Christopher had cracked and told y'all what had been signed that day in my office."

"Frank, I assure you we had no earthly idea. That day I only had the feeling there were entirely too many signatures required for the purchase of a house."

Everyone shared in a wholesome laugh before Frank replied, "Christopher had his wishes and as my client I only see them through, confidentiality clause included. Trust me, Christopher was a great judge of character, and I believe he made the best decision handing over the reins to y'all. He considered y'all family whom he loved dearly. May y'all still continue to carry on his vision for a better world."

"Frank, we will do our best to not fail,"

Manuel spoke sternly. "And would you mind retaining us as your clients?"

"It would be my pleasure," Frank said with a smile, "and you should know the last 24 hours have been nonstop with the media. '20/20' wants to run a two-hour special documenting Christopher's story, so you have a meeting set for Thursday at noon. Also, the Lifetime Network wants to produce a film about Christopher's life, so that meeting is on Friday at 2 p.m."

Allowing all that information to process in Manuel's mind, Frank took a deep breath before he continued, "Now that we got all that out of the way, let's eat. My beautiful wife has prepared a feast, hope y'all are hungry."

EPILOGUE

It was all so surreal for Manuel who had rose out of bed yesterday downtrodden and unsure of his family's future only to wake up today a multi-millionaire with a secure, successful life for his family and more money than he ever dreamed of in the bank account.

All along he realized Christopher was grooming him for this position. The many talks they shared and Chris even taking him to his tailor explaining to Manuel every man should have at least three suits in their closet—black, dark blue, and brown. That day Christopher purchased all three for Manuel, and today he chose to wear the dark blue to speak to the tenants of High Hopes where they were asked to convene in the restaurant after lunch was served.

Talks had been roaming the complex about who the new owner would be and will they be even close to as generous as Christopher had been. So, to settle everyone's nerves, Manuel had called for the meeting.

Before arriving at High Hopes Benina made it a point to have Manuel stop at the florist shop and purchase a dozen red roses and a dozen yellow roses then drive over to visit Chris and place the dozen red roses on the Leal headstone for his grandparents, placing the fresh dozen yellow roses on the Espinosa headstone for Chris and his family. Benina made a promise to Christopher in that moment to continue to keep his Saturday morning ritual of refreshing the roses for his loved ones, saying to Christopher through her heart, "Thank you for everything, and we'll be here Saturday."

With all three of their hearts in a knot from missing Christopher, they returned to the car with Mary jumping into the back seat with Cash. When Manuel started the car to leave it was in that instant that they received confirmation that Chris was in heaven and full of joy with his loved ones. The song that came on the radio was, "I Can Only Imagine" by Mercy Me, which happened to be Christopher's favorite. Riding that spiritual wave, they entered the restaurant feeling as though Christopher's spirit was with them.

Manuel had also invited Padre Evaristeo and Deacon Marco, LeAnn, and their teenage son and daughter. He figured they were as big a part of this charity work as anybody. Finding their way to the front, LeAnn and Benina greeted each other then carried on in conversation. Manuel approached Deacon Marco standing next to his kids. After shaking hands, Manuel looked at the kids and asked, "John and Rhylan, would you two be interested in making some money working on the weekends in the greenhouses?"

Looking to their father, Rhylan gave her undeniable face complete with big eyes and a pouty lower lip before politely asking, "Can we, daddy?"

All Marco could do was shake his head yes. He knew the instant she gave him that look he'd already lost the battle.

Turning back to Manuel they both exclaimed, "Yes, sir, we'll take the job."

"Good, we'll go over the details later," Manuel replied.

Everyone filed into the restaurant, brimming over capacity with the overflow standing along the walls.

Mary sat next to Rhylan so they could play with Cash as Manuel and Benina stood in the front with Frank, facing the tenants.

Frank opened with, "As you know, I have been a long-time friend and attorney for my beloved brother Christopher. For some time now many of us have lived life through tears due to his passing. As his attorney, I executed his last will and testament which transferred High Hopes into the power and complete control of Manuel and Benina Molina. With that being said, I will now let your new owners have the floor." Frank then stepped over to sit next to his wife.

Manuel took hold of his wife's hand as he addressed the crowd of unsure onlookers in a strong voice, "Our beloved brother Christopher has entrusted my beautiful wife and I to keep his legacy untainted. I once asked Chris why he named the apartments High Hopes, and he explained to me that those were the final precious words his daughter spoke to him."

Glancing at his stunning wife radiating from her pregnancy glow he then turned back to the tenants hanging on to his every word. "I assure you that everything will stay the same. My wife and I will run the complex as it always has been, to the letter, so as to respect Christopher's wishes. Also, we are here to serve and do our best to live as good Christians. Although Chris set the bar very high, we vow to continue to strive daily. With that being said, that makes me still your handyman and most importantly that means never changing the arrangements currently in place today or at any time in the future. And we look to y'all to continue to keep your promises to Christopher and pray daily."

With a sigh of relief he inquired, "Now, are there any questions?"

Quiet reverberated throughout the room, and in that moment everyone rose to their feet as a thunderous applause erupted inside the echoing restaurant. The tenants were wiping happy tears from their eyes in between claps.

The applause played to the beat of everyone's heart manifesting the love that creates the ripples that suppress the turbulent waves of life.

Benina took her husband's hand and placed it on her belly so Manuel could feel them jumping for joy. Smiling at his wife he said, "I'm a very blessed man."

It was Christmas morning and Manuel had taken his family to visit Christopher. Standing before the headstone he began to tell Chris how well the meetings with the tenants and

TV producers went while enjoying the gentle winter breeze on his face.

Benina was kneeling, refreshing the roses and fixing the Christmas decorations with Mary's help and Cash by Mary's side.

Mary looked over and saw a chubby tear roll down her mother's cheek. Hugging her around the shoulders Mary whispered, "Don't cry, momma, today is a good day. Christopher gets to go to Jesus' birthday party."

Taken aback as to how Mary's little world was so simple, she replied, "You're right, sweetheart. I didn't think about that."

In that moment Cash let out a soft bark capturing Mary's attention causing her to turn around, scooping him up in her arms, Cash licked her face and wagged his pudgy, furry tail as Mary exclaimed, "Oh, Cashie," before erupting into her childish giggle.